He made her feel really good...and that was bad.

Prince Stephan hadn't even been here twenty-four hours and already Mandy was getting in over her head. She had to put a stop to this attraction before it went any further. She had to remember that he wasn't just a good-looking man who set off fireworks in her body.

He was a prince—a wealthy, titled foreigner who'd come to steal her son.

Maybe she ought to write it a hundred times, the way she made her students write things over and over so they'd always remember them. Maybe if she never looked into his eyes again or listened to him talk or laugh or got close to him or thought about him...

Even if she could avoid him—and she didn't see how she could—getting him out of her thoughts was going to be a lot tougher.

Dear Reader,

Silhouette Romance blends classic themes and the challenges of romance in today's world into a reassuring, fulfilling novel. And this month's offerings undeniably deliver on that promise!

In *Baby, You're Mine*, part of BUNDLES OF JOY, RITA Award-winning author Lindsay Longford tells of a pregnant, penniless widow who finds sanctuary with a sought-after bachelor who'd never thought himself the marrying kind...until now. Duty and passion collide in Sally Carleen's *The Prince's Heir*, when the prince dispatched to claim his nephew falls for the heir's beautiful adoptive mother. When a single mom desperate to keep her daughter weds an ornery rancher intent on saving his spread, she discovers that *McKenna's Bartered Bride* is what she wants to be...forever. Don't miss this next delightful installment of Sandra Steffen's BACHELOR GULCH series.

Donna Clayton delivers an emotional story about the bond of sisterhood...and how a career-driven woman learns a valuable lesson about love from the man who's *Her Dream Come True*. Carla Cassidy's MUSTANG, MONTANA, Intimate Moments series crosses into Romance with a classic boss/secretary story that starts with the proposition *Wife for a Week*, but ends...well, you'll have to read it to find out! And in Pamela Ingrahm's debut Romance novel, a millionaire CEO realizes that his temporary assistant—and her adorable toddler—have him yearning to leave his *Bachelor Boss* days behind.

Enjoy this month's titles—and keep coming back to Romance, a series guaranteed to touch *every* woman's heart.

Mary-Theresa Hussey

Mary-Theresa Hussey
Senior Editor

Please address questions and book requests to:
Silhouette Reader Service
U.S.: 3010 Walden Ave., P.O. Box 1325, Buffalo, NY 14269
Canadian: P.O. Box 609, Fort Erie, Ont. L2A 5X3

THE PRINCE'S HEIR

Sally Carleen

Silhouette

ROMANCE™

Published by Silhouette Books

America's Publisher of Contemporary Romance

To Veda and Dee, the greatest in-laws ever.
Thank you for taking me into your family.

 SILHOUETTE BOOKS

ISBN 0-373-19397-1

THE PRINCE'S HEIR

Copyright © 1999 by Sally B. Steward

All rights reserved. Except for use in any review, the reproduction or utilization of this work in whole or in part in any form by any electronic, mechanical or other means, now known or hereafter invented, including xerography, photocopying and recording, or in any information storage or retrieval system, is forbidden without the written permission of the editorial office, Silhouette Books, 300 East 42nd Street, New York, NY 10017 U.S.A.

All characters in this book have no existence outside the imagination of the author and have no relation whatsoever to anyone bearing the same name or names. They are not even distantly inspired by any individual known or unknown to the author, and all incidents are pure invention.

This edition published by arrangement with Harlequin Books S.A.

® and TM are trademarks of Harlequin Books S.A., used under license. Trademarks indicated with ® are registered in the United States Patent and Trademark Office, the Canadian Trade Marks Office and in other countries.

Visit us at www.romance.net

Printed in U.S.A.

SALLY CARLEEN,

the daughter of a cowboy and a mail-order bride, has romance in her genes. Factor in the grandfather in 1890s Louisiana who stole the crowd at political rallies by standing on a flatbed wagon and telling stories, and it's no surprise she ended up writing romance novels.

Sally, a hard-core romantic who expects life and novels to have happy endings, is married to Max Steward, and they live in Missouri with their very large cat, Leo, and their very small dog, Cricket. Her hobbies are drinking Coca-Cola and eating chocolate, especially Ben & Jerry's Phish Food ice cream. Sally loves to hear from her readers: P.O. Box 6614, Lee's Summit, MO 64064.

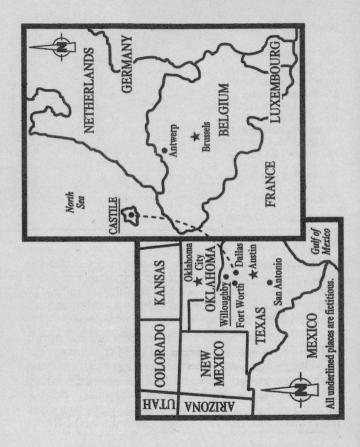

Chapter One

"Mama, Mama, Mama!" The screen door banged open and Joshua charged out as fast as his chubby little legs would carry him. At the same time a large dog, who appeared to be part bassett hound, part collie, part horse and all mongrel, gallumphed around the corner, his deep barking amazingly synchronized with Josh's excited shouts.

Mandy Crawford dashed to the porch, catching Josh as he started his usual tumble down the three front steps. He laughed as she lifted him into the air and whirled him around. "How's my boy? Can I have a kiss?"

He puckered up and planted a sloppy one on her cheek, then laughed some more.

The dog danced around them, woofing and waggling. Mandy set her son on one hip and reached down to pet the dog, scratching behind his floppy ear, as well as the one that always stood erect. "Good boy, Prince," she praised, knowing how desperately he wanted to jump on her but didn't since she was wearing her go-to-work clothes.

"Guboy," Josh echoed and leaned over to plant a kiss on the dog's head.

"Yuck! You've got a good heart, kiddo. Lousy judgment but a good heart."

With Prince temporarily quieted, she carried Josh back inside the house. "How about you? Have you been a good boy? Did you mind your Gamma today?"

"Gamma!" Josh wriggled down onto the faded area rug of the living room, wrapped a hand around Mandy's finger and launched into an enthusiastic but mostly incoherent monologue as he led her toward the kitchen. *Gamma*, *Nana* and *An Say See* were the only words she recognized—*Grandma*, Mandy's mother, *Nana*, Mandy's grandmother, and *Aunt Stacy*, Mandy's sister. The rest of the words were immaterial, anyway. Family was all that mattered.

"Mom! I'm home!" she called. "Do I smell fried chicken? Dad must be on his way. Is he closing the store early today? He should, as hot as it is."

"In the kitchen, sweetheart." Her mother's voice sounded oddly strained, and Mandy hesitated for a moment, fingers of fear tracing down her spine.

Josh tugged on her finger, and she tried to shrug off her unfounded fears. Ever since Gramps died three years ago, she'd been on edge, looking for trouble everywhere and all the time. She had to stop doing that. Life was good, and it was going to stay that way.

She let Josh lead her through the dining room and into the big old kitchen. Golden light streamed through windows on two sides, as well as through the screen door that led to the backyard. White-painted cabinets reflected and amplified the light, while yellow curtains, tied back at the sides of the windows, fluttered in the breezes created by the attic fan. It was Mandy's favorite room and the room where their extended family always seemed to congregate.

Standing beside the white enamel gas stove, Mandy's mother looked up from taking pieces of chicken out of the pan and laying them on a platter. There could be no mistaking the anxiety in her face, and Mandy's stomach clenched. Was her grandmother ill? Had something happened to the baby her sister-in-law was carrying?

As if drawn by a powerful magnet, her gaze moved to the rectangular oak table that filled one side of the room. A stranger rose from the chair between her sister Stacy and their grandmother.

It was hot in the room, even with the attic fan pulling in shade-cooled air, but the sober expressions on all the faces sent a chill down Mandy's spine.

"Mandy, we have a guest." Her mother's voice was tight, as if it would explode should she relax her grip on it.

Mandy looked more closely at the tall, elegant stranger. He was movie-star handsome with a square jaw and chiseled features. His hair was black like the summer sky just before dawn and his eyes were as blue as that same sky would be an hour later. For a flickering instant those eyes seemed as deep and as filled with tantalizing promises as that morning sky, but it must have been a trick of the bright light. In the next instant his gaze was glacial and distant, more like a January day when the winter stretched behind and ahead with no end in sight.

Mandy was both drawn to the man and disturbed by him.

His expression was set in stoic, controlled lines, his posture erect with a bearing that went beyond military—as if it were a part of him, something in his blood. His demeanor fit perfectly with his dark suit, white shirt and conservative tie.

No one dressed like that in late June in Texas.

Mandy's mother turned off the flame under the empty skillet and ran her hands down the front of her apron. "Mandy, this is Stephan Reynard. Mr. Reynard, my daughter, Mandy."

Stephan Reynard, Prince of Castile.

Her adopted son's biological uncle.

The smell of fried chicken became cloying and stuffy. The room blurred, with only Stephan Reynard's face in blindingly sharp focus.

She picked up Josh and held him tightly against her.

She should have recognized the resemblance to his brother immediately. Their features were similar, and he had the same stiff demeanor. But Lawrence Reynard's eyes had been gentle and sad, the eyes of a poet and a dreamer. Stephan was obviously neither.

"Hello, Ms. Crawford." His accent was the same…vaguely British with an underlying hint of something earthier, Scottish or Irish maybe.

"What do you want?"

Her sixteen-year-old sister stood and held out her arms. "Hey, Josh, why don't you come with Aunt Stacy? We can go outside and play with Prince for a little while."

Josh reached for his aunt, and Mandy reluctantly let him go.

Reynard arched a dark eyebrow. "Prince?"

"Our dog," Mandy said smugly. "He's the royalty around here."

"I see."

The screen door slammed behind Josh and Stacy.

"All right, what do you want?" Mandy repeated, more insistently this time.

"Mandy," her mother said sternly. "Where are your manners? Mr. Reynard is our guest."

"That's quite all right, Mrs. Crawford," the stranger said. "This isn't a social call."

"I didn't think it was."

"Perhaps we could go somewhere private to discuss this matter."

Mandy folded her arms across her chest. "This is as private as it gets. In fact, we really ought to wait until my dad and my brother, Darryl, and his wife, Lynda, get here, sort of a meeting of the entire royal assembly. Here in America the family is the ruling class, in case you haven't heard."

"Mandy," Rita Crawford said, moving over to wrap one arm around her daughter's shoulders, "why don't you take Mr. Reynard into the living room? It's much cooler in there."

Mandy shook her head. "No. This affects all of us. Doesn't it, Mr. Reynard?"

He inclined his head slightly and indicated an unoccupied seat across the table from him. "Very well. Then perhaps you'd care to take your seat in the 'royal assembly.'"

Mandy lifted an eyebrow. "Mother, why don't you go ahead and sit down. I'll remain standing. Isn't that appropriate in the presence of royalty?"

Reynard crossed his arms in imitation of her, but

she doubted that she had that same haughty air that enhanced his gesture and made it something more than a brave front. One corner of his mouth quirked upward in a movement that could have been the beginning of a smile on a face less stoic, and for the first time Mandy had a glimmering of understanding of the strong, inexplicable attraction Alena, her friend from childhood, must have felt for Lawrence. There was something compelling and dynamic about this man in spite of the circumstances.

"Only a moment ago you held the heir to the throne in your arms," he said. "I think we've gotten past formalities."

The heir to the throne. She'd known what was coming from the moment her mother announced this man's name, but hearing it put into words caused her stomach to clench into a hard, cold knot and her heartbeat to skip erratically.

It's all right, she tried to reassure herself. Everything about the adoption was legal, every *i* dotted, every *t* crossed.

But Lawrence had warned her that the island of Castile lived by the rules of its country, not by anyone else's, like the stupid decree that would make an illegitimate son heir to the throne if no legitimate heir existed.

But that wouldn't apply here.

"Lawrence did his duty. He went back home after Alena's death and married that Lady Barbara. They'll produce a legitimate heir. Give them a little time and leave Josh alone."

"You haven't heard about Lawrence's death?"

Lawrence's death? Mandy felt the blood drain from her face.

"Ms. Crawford? Are you all right?" The voice seemed to come from far away, part of the whirlwind of fear and confusion that spun through Mandy's head. If Lawrence was dead without leaving a legitimate son, that meant—

Stephan silently cursed his lack of tact as he hastily crossed the space separating him from Mandy and reached to catch her before she fainted.

As he grasped her slim shoulders, however, the color shot back into her pale cheeks. She took a deep breath, straightened and glared at him from eyes that were the same deep, glistening shade of green as the trees and grass they'd flown over on the last leg of the flight to Dallas.

He dropped his hands. "Are you all right?" he repeated, and was shocked to realize that he half wished she would say no, would give him an excuse to touch her, to support her and hold her willowy body in his arms, to lift that wild tangle of copper hair off her neck, run his fingers through the curls and see if they were truly composed of fire. The combination of jet lag and Texas heat was having a most peculiar effect on him.

"I'm fine." She moved away from him, over to the table to sit in the chair he'd indicated.

Just as well. He had more important things to do than lust after an attractive woman...especially a woman who was, without doubt, going to cause him all sorts of problems before this was over.

Mandy's grandmother took Mandy's smooth, slim hand in her wrinkled one and squeezed it in a comforting, protective gesture, and an unexpected, inexplicable spear of envy shot through Stephan's chest.

Ridiculous. He was tired from the long trip, worn

out already, though negotiations had barely begun. He was a member of the ruling family of Castile. They neither had nor could they afford to have pointless emotions.

"I'm sorry," he said. "I assumed you'd know about Lawrence's death. That was presumptuous of me. What makes for big news in our country likely doesn't merit a mention on the back page of the paper in your country."

"How did he die?" Mandy asked, her voice suddenly much softer than when she'd squared off against him a few moments ago.

"In an automobile crash. It happened two months ago."

"I'm sorry. He seemed to be a good person."

"Yes, he was. He would have been a good king."

"But now he's gone and you've come to take his son." She shook her head. "I can't believe he told you about Josh. He went to so much trouble to be certain your family would never find out."

Stephan returned to his chair and sat across the table from her. "Lawrence didn't tell us. The Taggarts were traveling in Europe when they saw the story. They contacted me."

"Alena's parents? Why would they do that?" Her eyes hardened to green ice and her lips tightened. "Oh, never mind. I can guess. They saw his picture and realized who Lawrence is. Was. Discovering that the father of their daughter's illegitimate child was a prince suddenly makes that child socially acceptable, even desirable."

Stephan considered Mandy's words. He'd always suspected the Taggarts might have had a hidden agenda in telling him…that it hadn't been just a case of ''doing their duty.'' He hadn't liked their smarmy attitudes and had hoped their story about Lawrence fathering a child would prove to be a fabrication, but it hadn't.

Rita Crawford set a glass of iced tea in front of Mandy, then took her seat at one end of the table. She was shorter than her daughter, and her hair was smooth and blond instead of wild and red, her eyes a tranquil blue. Yet even at a glance it was obvious the two were related. They both held their heads at that same proud angle that stopped short of being arrogant. Rita's eyes held the same fires as her daughter's, though Rita's were subdued, a lesson probably learned through experiences Mandy hadn't yet been through.

Vera Crawford, Mandy's grandmother, was a tiny woman with snow-white hair and a regal bearing that made her seem taller. Her eyes were a softer green than Mandy's, and she had a quiet, dignified beauty that transcended her years.

When Lawrence had first come to America to attend graduate school in Dallas, he'd regaled Stephan with stories of how different American women were, how independent...especially Texas women. They were, he'd said, all fluff and beauty and fragility on the outside, smiling and friendly, but their spines were tempered steel. No women in the world were prettier and none were tougher.

Now, flanked by three of them, Stephan truly understood his brother's words for the first time.

Mandy's grandmother gave her hand a final pat. ''Don't worry, baby. Everything's going to be all right.'' She turned her attention to Stephan. ''Now that Mandy's home, let's get on with things, Mr. Reynard, and discuss our options.''

There was only one option as far as he was concerned, but in the interest of diplomacy Stephan complied, anyway. He folded his hands on the smooth wood of the table, carefully avoiding the glass of cooled tea dripping condensation onto the table. When Rita Crawford had offered him tea, he'd expected it to be properly hot. Lawrence had failed to mention this peculiarity of Americans. Although, in this stifling heat, he could understand why they'd want their beverages cold.

''Shortly after Lawrence's death, my father received a letter from Raymond and Jean Taggart. According to this letter, they'd been traveling abroad when they saw my brother's picture in a newspaper and recognized him as their deceased daughter's lover, the father of her child. Naturally my father assumed it was a hoax, but he sent an investigator to check out the story and discovered evidence that Lawrence had indeed been involved with their daughter.''

''Lawrence and Alena loved each other very much,'' Mandy confirmed quietly. ''But of course he couldn't marry a commoner.'' Her voice rose slightly and she spat out the final word.

''Lawrence was the heir to the throne of his country. He had certain duties.''

''I know all about that garbage. Alena told me. And those duties didn't include making any of his own choices or falling in love, but he did both of those things in spite of his family.''

And look what came of his defying his duty, Stephan thought, but he refrained from saying it. Obviously Mandy Crawford approved of such rebellion.

"And Joshua is the result," he said instead.

"My son," she said firmly. "Everything about his adoption is totally legal. When he was born—" She bit her lush lower lip, and a film of moisture sprang to her eyes. To his amazement, Stephan felt a sudden wash of grief as if Mandy's emotions were so strong they reached from her all the way inside him.

She cleared her throat and continued. "I presume the Taggarts told you that Alena died giving birth to Josh. They were there when she said she wanted me to raise her son. Lawrence was there, too. Of course, the Taggarts didn't know he was a prince. Alena and I were the only ones who knew that. She told everyone else he was a poet. He was, you know. That's what he really wanted to do, not go back and spend his life in a fishbowl, doing and feeling only what your rules of royalty permitted him to do and feel."

"I know all about his hobby of writing poetry. My brother and I were very close." Stephan studied his clasped hands. Not all that close, evidently. Not close enough for Lawrence to tell him about Alena or Joshua. "He was instructed to keep his identity a secret. The idea was for him to attend your schools and study your culture without anyone realizing who he was. That was the only way he could hope to truly learn things. The poetry was a part of that disguise."

Mandy shook her head. "The poetry was part of Lawrence, the part that Alena fell in love with. Anyway, orders from the king or whatever had nothing to do with why Lawrence kept his identity secret from Alena's parents. The Taggarts may live in a million-dollar house in Dallas, excuse me, Highland Park—

that's much more prestigious, you know—but they both grew up right here in Willoughby. They were dirt poor until Alena's father hit it big wildcatting—"

"Wildcatting?" Stephan had an image of a man fighting with a wildcat. He'd heard some men wrestled alligators in America. Anything was possible over here.

"Oil wells. He made a bundle in oil, then invested it in the computer business. That's when they really hit it big. They moved to Dallas when Alena was thirteen, and they've been trying to break into society ever since. If they'd known Lawrence was a prince, they'd have gone totally bonkers, bragged to the world, conspired to somehow get their daughter married to him, and when she died, they'd have kept Joshua or given him to you. Whichever, neither Alena nor Lawrence wanted that for their son."

Stephan thought of the rough-cut couple he'd met, of their eager, obsequious attitudes and knew Mandy was right about them.

"Since they didn't know about Lawrence," she continued, "Alena's parents were only too happy to sign the adoption papers giving complete custody to me. It's all legal."

"But Lawrence didn't sign any adoption papers."

Her jaw tightened. "No. Alena didn't put his name on the birth certificate. It was something they both agreed on. Neither of them wanted to take any chances that their son would ever be discovered and have to live the way Lawrence had to live."

Stephan's mouth went suddenly dry. He reached for the glass of tea and sipped some of it. It didn't really taste very much like tea, but it was wet and cool. "As the heir to the throne, Lawrence led a life of luxury. He had everything he wanted."

Mandy's delicate chin firmed, and white pressure lines appeared around her full lips. "Your brother had everything he wanted except love. He found that when he met Alena, and that's the gift he wanted to give his son. My family may not have a lot of money. Joshua will never ride to school in a limousine or have a private tutor, but he has one thing neither of his parents ever had…plenty of love."

For a moment Stephan lost the thread of the conversation as he observed Mandy. What must it be like to experience such passion? Her emotions were completely out of control, swaying with the circumstances…anger, grief, defiance. It was something he'd been schooled from infancy not to do…and he was totally intrigued.

He drew himself up and drank more of the cool, sweetened tea. "If Joshua truly is Lawrence's son—"

Mandy shot up from her chair, her eyes blazing green fire, scorching him even from that distance. "*If* he's Lawrence's son? Exactly what is that supposed to mean?"

Again he found himself so fascinated by her passion he was momentarily speechless.

Vera Crawford stood, put a hand on her granddaughter's shoulder and stretched up to murmur something so low Stephan couldn't catch all the words.

Mandy nodded—reluctantly, he thought—then sank into her chair, leaned back and faced him defiantly. "If you have any doubts that Joshua is Lawrence's son, then maybe you'd just better haul your—"

"Mandy," the older woman interjected in a warning tone.

"Sorry, Nana." But he could tell she wasn't at all sorry for what she'd said or whatever she'd been about to say. She spoke the words to placate her grandmother, but continued to glare at him. "Perhaps it would be best if you took the next plane back to your big, cold palace and left us commoners to muddle along the best we can." Her amended suggestion was delivered in a fairly good imitation of his own speech patterns and he found himself wanting to smile in spite of the insult.

"A simple DNA test will resolve any doubts."

"I see." She clasped her hands on the table in front of her, again in imitation of him, and he braced himself for her next jab. She smiled tightly, her eyes still stormy. "You know, it just goes to show how deceptive appearances can be. I'd never have guessed until this very minute that you were dumb as dirt."

"Mandy," Vera Crawford cautioned again, though her tone was less stringent this time. She didn't really disapprove of her granddaughter's behavior.

"Dumb as dirt?" Stephan repeated.

"That's the only possible explanation for your assumption that I'd agree to a DNA test that would leave my son open to being shipped off to an island in the middle of the Atlantic Ocean where the people are more frigid than the climate!"

"If Joshua is Lawrence's son—and I believe he is or I wouldn't be here," he added hastily, "he is a prince, a descendant of a long line of kings. He should be permitted to come to his country and learn our customs and laws. One day, when my father steps down from the throne, Joshua will become a king. He'll be the ruling monarch of an entire country.''

"You know, if Lawrence couldn't marry Alena because of his duty to his country, it doesn't seem exactly fair to me that now her son should be forced into princehood.''

He smiled wryly at her naïveté. "Fair or not, that's the way it is. The decree dates from 1814.''

She waved a hand. "I know all about King Orwell and that stupid decree, and I don't care. The man's been dead almost two hundred years.''

"What decree, Mr. Reynard?'' Rita asked.

"King Ormond,'' Stephan corrected. "The Decree of Illegitimate Ascension. In the early 1800s King Ormond II produced one son who died in infancy and seven daughters. At his death, his illegitimate son by his acknowledged mistress came forth to claim the throne. Stafford was already popular with the court and the people. He was smart and well liked and he had a lot of good ideas for running the country. Even the queen approved of him, so the precedent was set. If Lawrence had produced a legitimate heir, Joshua would have been bypassed. But Lawrence did not. When my father steps down, Joshua will succeed to the throne. He may choose to abdicate that throne, but he should have the right to make that choice.''

Mandy lifted her glass of tea and took a deep, slow swallow. Her eyes were closed, the long lashes casting a shadow on her porcelain skin. She set the drink down carefully, drew a slim finger through the condensation on the outside of the glass and turned it a couple of times, her attention seemingly focused on the activity. Finally she again clasped her hands and looked up at him, and he saw that she was no longer angry but sad.

"It broke Lawrence's heart that he wouldn't be around to see his son grow up. When he put Josh in my arms, he cried."

She paused as if to let that phenomenon sink in. Stephan wasn't as shocked as he might have been, as he had been the first time he'd come upon his brother unexpectedly, a few months after his return from America, and found the tears streaming down his cheeks. Now he knew why.

"Your brother had a heart," she continued. "He cried when Alena died. He cried when he had to leave his son. Joshua has his father's heart and his mother's soul. He's a warm, caring little boy who will grow into a warm, caring man."

"He's a prince. He has royal blood in his veins. He belongs to his country."

"It's always bothered me a little," she went on as if he hadn't spoken, "that Joshua's family would never get to see him. My brother and his wife are expecting a baby in December, and I can't wait to see my niece or nephew. I'm almost as excited as they are. If someone told me I'd never get to hold that little baby, never get to see him grow up, I'd be devastated. When I walked in and saw you here, I was terrified that you'd be able to take Josh from me. I was terrified that you'd insist on holding him and you'd fall in love with him immediately and you'd tell me I had no right to keep your nephew from you. Lawrence said you were an all-right guy, so I was worried."

"Then you agree that the boy should be returned

to his family.'' Even as he spoke the words, he knew
they weren't true.

She arched an eyebrow. "But you didn't do any of
those things I'd expected and feared. You didn't show
any interest in Joshua because he's your nephew and
a neat little kid. Your only interest is in your stupid
country. You have no heart, no emotions. You're exactly the way Lawrence described the rest of his family. You're a part of the reason he didn't want the son
he loved to return there and be as lonely and miserable as your family made him.''

She slid her chair back and stood, then leaned over
the table and for one wild, heart-pounding moment,
he thought she was going to kiss him. Instead she
grabbed his tie by the knot and drew him closer. Her
face was mere inches from his, and he could see a
dusting of golden freckles that her makeup didn't
quite hide across her nose, could feel her breath warm
and sweet, but mostly he could see the flames that
blazed in her eyes. "You go on back to that country
and take over the throne as next in line of succession,
produce cold-hearted, unfeeling sons who can carry
on the family tradition, but don't you even think about
trying to take Joshua with you or I'll teach you the
meaning of the term *Texas wildcat,* and I'm not talking about anything to do with oil!''

She released her grip on his tie, whirled around and
strode out the back door, slamming it behind her.
"Would you like another glass of tea, Mr. Reynard?''
Rita asked.

Stephan blinked then suppressed an insane urge to
laugh. Her daughter had made an impassioned speech,
threatened him with the wrath of a Texas wildcat and
left. Even so, Rita Crawford observed the social

amenities. Perhaps Texas and Castile weren't so different after all.

"No, thank you," he said and rose from the table. "I must be leaving now. I know this has been a big shock for all of you. Here's the number of the hotel I'm staying at in Dallas. When you've had a chance to assimilate everything, please call me there."

Vera Crawford nodded. "We will, Mr. Reynard."

Stephan considered setting a time limit for them to call, warning them that if he didn't hear from them in three days, he'd contact them again.

But that was unnecessary. They'd call. They were honorable people.

He hadn't been prepared to like this family, but he did.

Mandy was wrong when she'd labeled him unfeeling. In the short time he'd been with her, she'd caused him to feel many things—respect, amusement, admiration and, last but not least, desire in the age-old way in which a man desires a woman. Royalty was not always free to indulge such desire, but that didn't mean he didn't feel it.

He, like Mandy's mother, realized the value of observing the amenities, of refusing to indulge emotions and let them influence one's life. As a member of the royal family—the future king, unless Joshua's claim to the throne could be validated—he could never afford that indulgence.

Yet as he stood and said goodbye to the Crawfords, and everyone smiled and mouthed the proper pleasantries, he had a very emotional feeling that before this was over, Mandy, with her fiery hair and blazing eyes, her porcelain skin brushed by freckles and her passion for everything, was going to test the limits of his restraint.

Chapter Two

Mandy leaned against the side of the house, half-hidden by a crepe myrtle bush, shaking in fear and anger as she watched Stephan's rental car drive away. How was it possible that her whole world could have changed so much in less than an hour?

Though she supposed she shouldn't be surprised. The last few years had been constant upheaval...leaving her small hometown, Willoughby, for college in Dallas, fifty miles away, renewing her friendship with Alena, then her grandfather's death three years ago followed closely by Alena's death, adopting Josh and moving back to Willoughby. She'd thought she could regain stability by returning to the small town and the family she'd once wanted to leave. And she had regained that stability for a while. She'd traded in her MBA to teach first-grade children, some belonging to her former classmates.

Except for her grandfather and her best friend being gone, the time since she'd come back had been like a return to her childhood when she was surrounded by love and everything was secure and unchanging. She'd been given a second chance, and this time she truly appreciated what she had. This time she was holding on with both hands and not about to let it get away from her.

Only a few hours ago she'd left to do her morning of volunteer work at the library, confident that things would be the same when she returned. Then she'd come back and walked into the home where she'd lived since she was a child, where she'd always felt safe, into the kitchen where she'd eaten breakfast that very morning with the people she loved.

But in that kitchen, sitting at that same table, she'd seen Stephan Reynard.

And she had a horrible feeling that her life would never be the same no matter how tightly she tried to hold on to the status quo.

The worst thing wasn't even that he wanted to take Josh. That was unthinkable, of course, but even worse was that she was inexplicably, insanely attracted to the man who wanted to steal her son, the brother of the man who'd caused her best friend's death.

For some reason she'd never be able to understand, her hormones had turned on her and focused their attention on this enigmatic man who was the antithesis of everything she wanted out of life. He had wealth and power and that always spelled heartache. If she needed any confirmation of that fact of life... and she didn't...all she had to do was look at Alena's life, especially after she became involved with this man's brother.

Stephan Reynard was from another country. Not just another city an hour's drive away, but a completely different country, thousands of miles away in distance and lifestyle.

And he was the enemy, the man who thought that country had a claim on her son, who wanted to yank him away from her and from the life she'd so carefully constructed for him.

Yet as much as she feared Stephan and hated him, just as much was she drawn to him. There was something about him, some banked fire in his eyes, something predatory about the way he moved, something primitive buried beneath the layers of civilization and conservative clothing that reached to a part of her she hadn't even known existed before…and really didn't want to know about now.

When he'd callously announced Lawrence's death, she'd been completely disconcerted, not only because she'd liked Lawrence and had been shocked at the news, but also because that meant Stephan had a legitimate reason to take her son. The room had started to spin about her. Stephan must have spotted her weakness, and he'd rushed over to her. For one insane instant she'd wanted to collapse into those arms and be held against that wide chest, to free those uncivilized urges she somehow knew he possessed.

Fortunately she'd recovered her good sense before doing anything that stupid and had not, she hoped, given him any sign of her absurd reaction.

When she'd grabbed him by that ridiculous tie and invaded his space to issue her warning, she'd been fighting dual urges to use that tie to choke him or to pull his lips to hers. Even now she could remember the sizzle that had seemed to pass from his body to hers, though they hadn't actually touched physically.

Even now his elusive scent that was both foreign and familiar, civilized and wild, tantalized her memory.

She snapped a leaf off the bush beside her and crumpled it in her fingers. Her hormones must have gone into overdrive, focusing on the first attractive man they spotted, causing her to attribute to that man all sorts of traits that he didn't possess. Stephan Reynard was a stuffy, snobbish, arrogant prince who wanted to take her son.

She had to shove her rebellious hormones back into their cells and launch a crusade against Stephan Reynard. She had to protect Alena's son—her son now—keep her promise to Alena and Lawrence and keep her family intact.

She drew in a deep breath, determinedly pulling in the familiar scents of honeysuckle and trees and dust in an effort to drive out Stephan's enigmatic, enticing scent.

Spine straight and head high, she returned to the backyard where Stacy, Josh and Prince were involved in one of Josh's favorite games. Stacy threw Prince's bone, then Josh raced with the dog to see who would retrieve it.

"I'm going in to talk to Mom and Nana, Stacy. Would you keep Josh out here for a little while longer?"

Stacy tossed the bone, then when Josh and Prince ran after it, she turned to Mandy, a worried frown marring her young features. "What's going to happen, Sis?"

"Nothing. We'll figure out some way to deal with this." She had no idea what that way might be, but she would find it. She couldn't conceive of anything else.

Josh charged back, jubilantly clutching the plastic bone and chattering happily.

"Good boy!" Stacy approved. "See how much easier it is to carry it in your hand than in your mouth?"

Mandy scooped him up and gave him a big hug, loving him so much it was almost painful. Josh wrapped his chubby arms about her neck and hugged her back, gave her a sloppy kiss, then demanded to be allowed down again so he could play with Prince. She set him on his bare feet and he scampered away.

"He doesn't appreciate how much he's loved because that's all he's ever known," Mandy said. "That's the way it ought to be, and it's not going to change."

"I'm with you all the way," Stacy replied.

Mandy went back inside to her mother and grandmother who sat at the table, waiting for her.

"We got problems," she said.

Her grandmother grinned wryly. "You always did have a talent for understatement."

She flopped into the chair beside her. "Any thoughts on what we're going to do?"

Nana shook her head. "When you told us you were adopting Josh, you didn't tell us about that decree of illegitimate ascension."

Mandy sighed. "It didn't seem important. I thought Lawrence would marry the woman his parents had picked out for him and have lots more sons. It's the male who determines the sex, you know, so the odds were pretty good on that one. I certainly had no idea the Taggarts would ever in a million years find out about Lawrence. It's not like they would be on a guest list for the palace ball and recognize him."

The front door slammed. "Hi, honey! I'm home!"

"In the kitchen, Dan!" her mother called.

Mandy had to fight the urge to jump up, run to her father and throw herself in his big, capable arms, the way she had done when she was a little girl, when he could make everything all better with a kiss. "You're going to wish you'd stayed at the hardware store!" she shouted instead.

Dan Crawford appeared in the doorway, a large, smiling man with auburn hair fading to a lighter color and streaked with white. He took one look at the three of them and his smile vanished, concern furrowing his brow instead. "What's wrong? Has something happened to Lynda and the baby?"

"No, they're fine," Rita assured him. "Sit down, dear. We need to have a family meeting."

Dan took a seat at the table and listened quietly while Mandy told him the whole story.

"We need a plan of action," she concluded. "I don't think this is going to go away like the chicken pox did."

Dan Crawford leaned back and exhaled a long sigh. "What did this Stephan Reynard say he plans to do next?"

"He didn't say," Rita replied. "He's staying at a hotel in Dallas and we're to phone him there after we've had time to discuss everything."

"There's nothing to discuss," Mandy said adamantly. "Joshua's my son now. Both his parents wanted him to have the kind of life I had, not the kind they had."

"Stephan Reynard is Joshua's uncle," her father said, his voice quiet but resolute. "He may not have any legal rights, but don't you think he's entitled to some kind of relationship with his nephew? Someday Joshua's going to want to know about his heritage."

"Stephan Reynard doesn't want a relationship with his nephew. He wants to steal him and turn him into a carbon copy of himself, and we can't let him do that. Josh would be just as unhappy in that role as Lawrence was."

She rose, unable to sit still any longer, and paced across the kitchen, then turned around and leaned back against the cabinet as if for support. "When I was little, I envied Alena. She had so many toys and clothes and her own suite of rooms. But she always wanted to come to our house to play. I didn't understand that. Then I went to Dallas to go to school and we got really close again and she told me she'd been lonely and envied my family."

She wrapped her arms about herself and smiled weakly. "That was the first time I'd been away from you all. I used to think it would be wonderful to have a place of my own, central heat and air, my own private bathroom. Well, it wasn't. I never told you how much I missed all of you because you were so pleased about my getting that scholarship and going to school. But I did. Something terrible. If I hadn't had Alena, I wouldn't have stayed even that first semester. When Gramps died, it really hit me how valuable you all are to me. Then Alena died, too, and Lawrence put that tiny baby in my arms, and it was like everything shifted and I totally understood. I knew that making lots of money and having lots of *things* the way Alena had always had was not what I wanted. I'd had the world and given it up. I couldn't get everything back. Gramps was gone. But I could reclaim the rest of my life, and I wanted Josh to have what you gave me, such a good life that he'd never comprehend loneliness. And he does. Where his ancestors came from doesn't matter. Love is the only heritage that matters.''

"You're almost right, baby," her grandmother said. "Love is the most important, but do you really want to deprive Joshua of knowing about his biological heritage? You're always saying how it makes you feel connected to live in the house built by your ancestors. Shouldn't Josh at least know about his?''

Mandy sighed in resignation. Her grandmother was right. Even if she'd had a choice...and she suspected that fighting an entire country didn't give her one... she wouldn't be able to keep Stephan away from his nephew.

"I'll call Stephan Reynard tomorrow," she agreed dully.

"You must invite him to stay with us," her mother said.

A rush of hot blood surged through Mandy at the thought of Stephan Reynard sleeping under the same roof with her. "Absolutely not!''

Rita Crawford ignored her daughter. "I'm sure he can't be comfortable in that hotel. I'll clean and air the guest room on the third floor.''

"I've got a real strong feeling that Stephan Reynard, Prince of Castile, is quite comfortable in that luxury hotel with room service and valet service and maid service. No way is he going to want to move from there into a third-story room in an old house that doesn't even have elevators or central air or chocolates on the pillows at night.''

"Mandy," her grandmother said, "your mother's right. When Mr. Reynard has a chance to see how happy Joshua is with us and how much we love him, he'll realize he can't take him away."

"It's the polite thing to do and the smart thing," her father said firmly. "You're outvoted, baby doll."

There was a down side to living with an extended family, Mandy thought grimly. Like being outvoted.

"Fine. I'll invite him because it's the polite thing to do and because you all insist, but I don't think he'll come."

Maybe he'd be so embarrassed when he refused that he'd stay away from her family.

It wasn't much, was pretty lame, actually, but it was the only hope she had at the moment.

Heaven help her and her renegade hormones if he accepted.

Stephan had a restless night. Jet lag. Traveling to a time zone six hours behind his. That's all it was. His troubled dreams about the Crawford family, Mandy Crawford in particular, were caused by the jet lag.

He rose early, awakening as usual just before dawn as if the energy of the sun was so strong it made sleep impossible and urged him to be up and busy doing things. He showered, dressed and ordered room service, then stared out his window at the Dallas skyline.

Dallas was a big, fast-paced, modern city, the complete opposite of everything in Castile. Lawrence had brought back glowing reports from America and ideas for bringing Castile into the twenty-first century. Though he'd been fascinated with both New York City and Dallas, he'd expressed a decided preference for Dallas. After learning about Alena and the child,

Stephan had wondered if Lawrence's perceptions had been tainted.

Stephan's own education and travels had focused on the capitals of Europe, and, in spite of Lawrence's reports, he'd halfway expected to find Dallas uncivilized and overrun with cattle and cowboys. But he had to admit he'd been favorably impressed. The vitality and energy of the city were almost palpable, yet the people, like the Crawfords, were polite and friendly.

He certainly hadn't expected to like the Crawfords. The Taggarts had described their socio-economic status as "low class," "dead broke," "the whole family living in a run-down old house." He hadn't liked or trusted the Taggarts when they'd traveled to Castile for an interview with the king after their claim had proven accurate. He hadn't been sure how much to believe of their analysis of the situation concerning the Crawfords. Nevertheless, he had fully expected to find Lawrence's son living in squalor.

He'd been prepared to march in boldly, demand a DNA test from people who would, the Taggarts assured him, be only too happy to relinquish the infant prince into his custody in exchange for a sizable deposit in their bank account. He had certainly not been prepared for the immaculate old house or for the cultured, well-mannered Crawford family who obviously adored Lawrence's son.

And nothing could have prepared him for Mandy Crawford.

This matter, which should have been simple and easily resolved, had become quite complicated.

He turned away from the window, folded his arms and took in a deep breath. If he was completely hon-

est with himself, he'd have to admit that it wasn't the
jet lag at all that had kept him awake most of the
night. It was the situation he'd unexpectedly come
into. Specifically, it was one tall, slender woman with
wild red hair, flashing green eyes and a burning passion that seemed to extend to everything around her,
a woman he'd touched briefly when he'd thought she
was going to faint, then been inches away from when
she'd gotten in his face to warn him to leave her son
alone, a woman who stayed in his mind far more viv-
idly than any of the women he had touched much
more intimately through the years.

The phone rang and he knew it was Mandy, as if
his thoughts of her could have compelled her to
call…or as if her thoughts of calling him, of picking
up the phone, of thinking about what she might say
to him, were so strong, so passionate, that they
reached across the miles.

He snatched up the phone on the first ring, then,
irritated at his own eagerness, answered with a crisp
"Hello."

"Stephan Reynard?" Mandy spoke crisply also,
but still her soft voice reminded him of the way the
wind had breathed through the leaves of the big trees
at her house yesterday.

"Speaking," he replied, ignoring his fanciful
thoughts.

"This is Mandy Crawford."

"I know."

"We need to talk."

"Yes, we do."

"When would be convenient for you?"

"I'm at your disposal."

"Good. That means we can work around my

schedule.'' Her tone was confrontational, but Stephan found himself smiling. Texas women were definitely different from any he'd known before. Or maybe it was just that Mandy Crawford was different from anyone he'd known before.

''I'll be delighted to work around your schedule. What time is convenient for you?''

''How about two o'clock in the lobby of your hotel?''

It was a good choice for him, his turf rather than hers, and it was air-conditioned. After experiencing the Texas heat yesterday, that was most definitely a positive aspect. Yet he felt a vague disappointment that he wouldn't be returning to the hot, stuffy old house overrun with the Crawford family.

''Two o'clock is fine. The restaurant here is quite good. Will you join me for a late lunch?''

''My family and I eat lunch together after we get home from church.''

Stephan flinched. That comment put him in his place, let him know that he had no part in her family, including any part in the child's life. He could almost see her as she spoke, her chin tilted upward, eyes glowing with righteous fervor. He supposed he should find her defiance upsetting or, at best, amusing, but somehow he didn't. Somehow he found it admirable and endearing.

''I'll see you at two,'' he agreed.

He hung up the phone, somehow reluctant to break the connection even as he was a little aghast at how much he was looking forward to seeing her again. This was purely business, of course. He would not— could not—become personally involved to any degree. That sort of thing only caused problems. He'd always known that, been taught that from the cradle, and Lawrence's fiasco certainly proved it.

He couldn't avoid seeing Mandy Crawford again, but he could stop himself from looking forward to it. He knew how to control his emotions.

Mandy stood in the elegant lobby of the hotel, tapping her foot on the marble floor. Two o'clock and no prince. She'd give him the benefit of the doubt. Maybe his watch was slow. Maybe they didn't value punctuality in Castile. But five more minutes and she was out of there.

If he couldn't even be on time, that surely showed he wasn't all that interested in Josh. Or maybe it just showed his complete disrespect for her and her family. After all, they weren't royalty, not even by the American standards of wealth and success. But they were a family, and that counted for more. If he measured them differently, then he was using the wrong standards.

"Ms. Crawford. How nice to see you again."

She whirled at the deep, mellow sound of his voice, the rounded, elegant intonation of his words with that underlying hint of uncivilized ancestry.

And somehow all her righteous anger melted in the depths of his eyes and the width of his smile.

"You're late," she snapped, irritated at herself, and taking it out on him. Why not? He was the cause of her problems, wasn't he?

He glanced at his gold watch then arched a dark eyebrow. "One minute."

"Oh. Well." She shifted her shoulder bag.

"Would you join me in a cup of tea? As I mentioned, the restaurant is quite nice."

"Yes, thank you. That would be...nice."

He extended one hand in the direction she should go, then placed the other in the vicinity of her waist, almost but not quite touching. She sucked in a quick breath. He might as well be touching her. She could feel the pulsating, vibrant heat from his hand through her cotton dress, and it was all she could do to refrain from letting that heat pull her to him, to lean slightly backward and feel his hand on her body.

She was being ridiculous again, letting her hormones control her brain, take over her imagination.

She walked faster, marching past the huge columns and into the restaurant that would have made Julius Caesar and his cronies feel right at home. A glass wall on one side looked onto a pool surrounded by lush vegetation. *Quite nice* was a gross understatement.

Mandy experienced a single, quick stab of anxiety that she was completely out of her element, in over her head. Without any overt effort, this man compelled her. He was a prince, born to rule. He had money and power. He was right at home in luxurious surroundings like this hotel. He was dangerous.

She sank into the chair the waiter held for her and gave herself a mental slap. She couldn't afford to lose her perspective. This man had money and power, but she had family and love. *He* was in over *his* head.

She started to order a glass of iced tea, then changed it to a cup of hot, the same as Stephan requested.

"Hot sounds good," she said after the waiter left. "It's chilly in here." She rubbed the goose bumps that covered her bare arms. The sleeveless summer dress she'd worn to church was not adequate for the frigid air of the hotel. Stephan, of course, wore a dark suit, white, long-sleeved shirt and a tie, just as he had the day before and probably the day before that. Maybe he even slept in them.

No....

Sitting across from him, surrounded by pompous elegance, she was again struck by the intense savagery that seemed to lie just beneath his cultured veneer. With a clarity she didn't want, she knew this man slept in the nude.

She folded her hands on the white tablecloth, shoved aside that image and prepared to launch into battle. "Well, Mr. Reynard, or should I call you Your Highness or maybe just Prince?" She bit back a nervous giggle at that thought. *Yo, Prince! Sit, Prince! Stay, Prince! Good boy!*

He smiled. "Prince? The name you reserve for your dog? I'm flattered. But I insist you call me Stephan. Your country isn't as formal as mine."

"Oh, are we playing by my country's rules?"

"I think that's appropriate considering we're in your country."

"Good. My country doesn't recognize royalty. Josh was born in this country, to an American citizen. That means he's an American, and by our rules, he can't be a prince. That should settle our differences."

He smiled again and inclined his head in a slight bow. "Touché. Legally speaking, I'm sure you're correct. Nevertheless, Lawrence's son is the heir to the throne of my country."

"So? You never did answer my question. What do you want? Do you think I'm going to just turn him over to you, let you take my son...and he is my son under the laws of my country...let you take him thousands of miles away, raise him in a style his biological father hated? Ruin his life?''

"When I first scheduled this trip over here," he said, his voice quiet and noncommittal, "I had planned to return with Lawrence's son—''

"Stop calling him that," she interrupted. "He's not just your brother's son. He's a person. He has a name. Joshua.''

"Of course," he acceded. "I had planned to return with *Joshua* so that he could be raised in the palace and trained for the duties he will one day undertake.''

"Your mom and dad anxious to meet their grandson, are they?" she asked sarcastically.

He stared at her blankly for a moment, his expression confused as if he were trying to comprehend a question couched in a foreign language, then a flash of something else swept across his features. He blinked and it was gone, but just for an instant Mandy could have sworn she glimpsed sadness in his winter eyes. "Of course the king and queen are anxious to meet Lawrence's—to meet Joshua.''

"They don't want to meet Joshua. They want to meet the heir. That's all he is to any of you. Alena told me how Lawrence was raised. One nanny after another, practically having to request an audience to see his parents. How can you want to do that to a little boy?''

"He's a prince. He has obligations and duties to his people.''

The waiter returned with their teas, and Mandy busied herself adding sugar and lemon, trying to keep her fingers from trembling visibly. She wasn't going to get anywhere in a head-to-head battle with this man. All she was doing was letting her anger and fear spoil her judgment. She had to be as cool as he was, fight him at his own game...and win. For Joshua's sake, she had to win.

"This is a beautiful hotel," she said, searching for a neutral subject to give her a chance to regain her equilibrium. "Is it similar to the hotels in your country?"

Stephan looked around him. "The service, yes. But we are a small country and very steeped in tradition. Even our renovated hotels are about a hundred years behind yours. That was why the king sent Lawrence to America, so he could bring back progressive ideas. We're badly in need of change." He smiled wryly. "As the world heads into the twenty-first century, we've barely entered the twentieth."

She didn't miss the fact that he had, for the second time, referred to his father only as "the king." After what Alena had told her about Lawrence's childhood, she wasn't surprised. Perhaps Stephan was more like his brother than he'd first appeared. Perhaps the fact that he had no real family had occasioned that brief glimpse of sadness she'd seen earlier when she'd mentioned his parents.

"So Lawrence came to America to study progress, and you went to Europe to study history."

He nodded and sipped his tea.

"Don't you have a sister? Alena mentioned a sister."

His taut features seemed to relax infinitesimally, and his long fingers curled around the small cup. He had a soft spot beneath that rigid exterior after all. "Yes, I have a younger sister, Schahara."

"And where did she go for her studies?"

"She's a woman. The queen taught her all she needs to know at home."

Mandy set her cup on the table so hard a bit of tea sloshed out onto the immaculate white linen. "Excuse me?"

He chuckled. "I told you we needed to learn about progress. In defiance of tradition, my sister has traveled extensively all around the world on her own accord. She's really the one with the ideas on how to bring about the progress we so desperately need. She's already computerized the household records and constantly monitors world happenings by using the Internet."

"You have computers in your country? Computers aren't nineteenth century."

He laughed then, a delicious, low sound that traveled from her ears through her body like a curling, rhythmic wave. "We're not completely primitive. We have electricity and indoor plumbing and even computers, though only the wealthy can afford the luxuries like televisions and computers, and many of our people still live without most or any of the modern conveniences."

"That's part of the changes you want to make?"

"A big part. As I said, Schahara has many plans already mapped out. The king wants to maintain the status quo and doesn't give much heed to her ideas. However, she will be an excellent adviser to the present king's successor."

"And who will that be if Joshua doesn't...um—"

"If he doesn't return to Castile? Then I'll succeed to the throne."

That was the first encouraging bit of news she'd

heard since yesterday. "Well, so, wouldn't you like to be king?"

"It's not a question of whether I'd *like* to be the king. It's a question of who is the rightful heir to the throne."

"But you would like to be king."

"I neither like nor dislike the idea. It's a duty. If I have to perform it, I will, of course. But Lawrence's son is—"

"Joshua! His name is Joshua Crawford and he's my legally adopted son and you can't just throw him over your shoulder and take him off to another country." She bit her lip and looked down at the table. She was losing control again.

"I assure you, I have no intention of doing that." And he was completely in control, as always. "Once I met your family, I realized my original plans couldn't happen. You and I must find a compromise. I've given it quite a bit of thought and have decided perhaps both sides would be best served if we could work out an alternating schedule of living arrangements while he's underage, say six months a year in each country. That would give him a chance to be with your family as well as to learn about his country."

Mandy's stomach clenched. She gazed at Stephan in horror. "Divide him up? Tear him in two? Keep him so unbalanced he never feels at home anywhere, never has a chance to settle into either life?"

"Very well, then what do you suggest?"

It was, she decided, time to play her trump card. She had no other choice. She leaned back in her chair and tented her fingers on the tabletop. "I suggest you get to know him and let him get to know you before we make any decisions."

"That sounds fair."

"My mother's cleaning out the guest room for you even as we speak. You can move in tonight and start getting to know your nephew immediately."

His eyes widened, and for a moment those banked fires she'd imagined she'd seen in his dark gaze sprang to life as awareness surged across the table between them, tingling along her skin and dancing around her breasts.

She swallowed hard and fumbled with her cup, lifting it to her lips and trying to focus on the lukewarm liquid inside rather than Stephan's scorching gaze.

When she looked back, the distant January skies had returned to that gaze and once again she had to wonder if her imagination and overactive hormones had created a delusion.

"Very well," he said. "I'll check out of here and move into your guest room tonight for a two-week stay. That should give us time to make all the necessary decisions." Despite his proper language, his voice was husky and raw and she recalled her earlier certainty that he slept in the nude.

And he'd be sleeping under the same roof as she tonight.

Chapter Three

A number of factors had compelled Stephan to agree to Mandy's offer—or, more precisely, her challenge—for him to stay in her home. A large part of that decision had sprung unexpectedly from her comments about the way both he and Lawrence had been raised. Until she brought it up—threw it in his face, to be precise—he'd shoved to the back of his mind the way he and his brother and sister had huddled together when they were small children in a big, cold palace, ignored by their parents, clinging to each other. Lawrence had been the oldest and the first to recognize that dependence on the succession of nannies was futile. He'd shared that knowledge with his younger siblings, pointing out that they were royalty and couldn't afford to become attached to people.

Certainly Stephan realized that a prince had to be rational and avoid sentimentality. Even so, he couldn't simply take this child off to a foreign country and into the midst of strangers. It was imperative he get to know him first. Joshua wouldn't even have a brother or sister to cling to.

But there was more to his decision, something elemental underlying the battle he and Mandy were waging, something that tugged at him and drew him to her, something that stirred his blood and tightened his groin. That *something* had him speeding to her house with his suitcases in the trunk of his rental car, anticipation and dread sharing equal space in his chest.

When he pulled up in front of the big old house, he wasn't surprised to see the entire family sitting on the porch, drinking that strange iced tea. Mandy, her mother, grandmother, younger sister, a tall older man with reddish hair streaked with white, who must be Mandy's father, a younger man with auburn hair who was holding hands with a smiling brunette—undoubtedly the brother and his wife—along with Joshua and the mongrel they called Prince. At least he didn't have to worry about giving in to any of those lustful tuggings for Mandy, not with that many people around.

Mandy separated from the group—reluctantly, he thought—and came to meet him. Joshua charged out and greeted him like a long-lost friend, tugging on his pants leg and chattering.

Stephan looked down at the boy and tried to think of how he should act with him, what he should do. Sweat broke out on his forehead, and it wasn't just from the heat of the day. He knew how to entertain kings and queens and foreign diplomats, but he had no clue what to say to this small child who couldn't even speak recognizable English.

"He's never met a stranger," Mandy said. Joshua lifted one small hand and Stephan cautiously enfolded it in his, marveling at the feel of the tiny fingers. Joshua led him up the sidewalk.

A shadow crossed Mandy's face as she looked down at the boy holding his hand. Doubtless she saw this as a step in the process of losing her adopted child. He did feel compassion for her situation, but there was nothing he could do to change the facts.

She graciously introduced her father, who insisted that Stephan call him Dan, then her brother, Darryl, and his wife, Lynda. Everyone welcomed him as if he were an honored guest rather than an interloper. In some of their customs, he thought for the second time, this family in Texas and his own family were not so far apart. Except no young child in his family would be permitted to take the hand of a guest. No young child in his family would look so happy and carefree.

"I'll show you to your room," Mandy offered, moving toward the door.

"Your bags in the car?" her father asked.

"Yes. I'll get them."

"I'll help."

"Thanks, but I only have two. I can manage."

Dan clapped him on the back. "It's a long climb up those two flights of stairs when you're carrying something heavy. I should know. Rita's had me carry at least a thousand tons of stuff up there over the years."

"Dan!" his wife chided, but she smiled along with the others, and he sensed a closeness between Mandy's parents.

The distance between their two countries was widening again.

He and Dan retrieved the bags, and Mandy led the

way up a wide, curved staircase. The wood on the steps was worn in the middle from many years of use, but it was clean and polished, and windows let in light and air at every turn.

Yesterday he'd been extremely tense and focused, but even so, the frustrated architect in him had noticed the successful blend of practicality and beauty in this house...features such as high ceilings to let the oppressive heat rise, opposing windows to create cross currents of air, curtains of open-weave fabric that kept out sunlight but let in air, covered porches on each side of the house to shade open doorways that were appealing as well as functional. There were also some things that were merely beautiful...crown molding in all the rooms, arched doorways, carved pillars on the porch. Now he found himself eagerly anticipating a view of the Crawfords' guest quarters.

He wasn't disappointed. The large room had windows on two sides, white lace curtains billowing and falling in the breezes, a large four-poster bed with a crocheted spread and a vase filled with fresh flowers sitting on the crocheted scarf that covered the top of a large dresser. The room—this house—was like everything else he'd seen in Texas...big, spacious, open and honest.

"Get unpacked and make yourself comfortable," Dan said. "Bathroom's right next door. You've got the whole floor to yourself. Dinner'll be ready in about an hour. Rita's making pot roast. Hope you're hungry!"

He left, but Mandy lingered, smoothing the spread, straightening the pillows. "I know it's a little feminine, but Nana made the spread and all the scarves and doilies. She likes to crochet."

"It's very nice." He was suddenly aware that the two of them were alone in a room with a bed. That sort of thing would never happen in his country, where the proprieties were more strictly observed. Of course he had no intention of so much as touching her, but the very idea set his blood to rushing past his ears, to pooling in his groin.

"This is where Nana and Granddad stayed until he died a few years ago. After that, she said the stairs were getting to be a little too much for her, but I think it just felt too lonely. She wanted to be down with her family."

She turned to look at him. As if she could read his mind—or his libido, to be precise—her eyes widened in surprise, then the lids drifted languidly half-closed, smoky with that same awareness he felt. For an instant out of time his gaze held hers while a sexually charged tension crackled between them. A sweet, wild scent touched his nostrils, and he wasn't sure if it belonged to some kind of flower and was blown in through the open windows or if it belonged to Mandy, but he did know that if he ever smelled that scent again, it would conjure up images of this woman.

She licked her lips, the action leaving them moist and slightly parted, and he'd never wanted to kiss anyone so badly in his life.

"If you need anything—" She blushed, apparently noticing the double entendre inherent in her words. "There are towels and soap and all that in the bathroom."

She turned slightly to point down the hall, and a ray of sunlight touched her, setting her hair ablaze and accenting the translucence of her porcelain skin. The stark white of the sundress she wore gave her shoulders and arms a creamy glow. The dress was cut just low enough to tease and tantalize with hints of the roundness of her breasts, and he could too easily imagine the feel of them in his hands...soft and warm and heavy, the nipples large and rosy and pebbling at his touch.

If you need anything. He needed her. He needed to touch her, hold her against him, make love to her.

He needed to get back into control, to force his brain to override his libido.

But that certainly wasn't what he *wanted* to do.

"Thank you," he managed to say, and was surprised to hear his voice come out sounding relatively normal. Years of training, he supposed. "I'll let you know if I—" he swallowed hard "—need anything."

She gave one curt nod, then whirled away and darted from the room, which seemed vast and empty with her gone. His legs oddly shaky and his heart pounding, he moved across the room to sit in the wooden rocking chair.

From the time they were children, he, Lawrence and Schahara had been taught to focus on the situation at hand, to be logical, to act and react in a rational, intelligent manner, always to remember that they were members of the royal family, that the rest of the country was counting on them. But nothing in that training had prepared him for a situation like this, for the way Mandy Crawford's hair blazed in the sunlight, the creamy slope of her shoulders, the rounded curve of her breasts, her wide, generous Texas mouth that begged to be kissed.

He'd seen the disaster that resulted from Lawrence's getting involved with an American, forgetting who he was and *falling in love.* Lawrence had forgotten what they'd learned as children, that royalty couldn't become attached to anyone. This entire problem had resulted because of Lawrence's indiscretion. Stephan was not going to fall into that trap, no matter how tantalizing Mandy might be, no matter how much his body begged to be trapped with hers.

Mandy set the last plate on the dining room table, concentrating fiercely on not dropping it. Her hands were shaking and her mouth was dry from her encounter with Stephan Reynard. She'd known inviting him to stay was a bad idea. He hadn't been here an hour and already he'd bonded with Joshua and with her hormones, and it could only get worse. Though darned if she knew how!

"Sweetheart," her mother said, "we can use either the good china or the everyday china, but I don't think we ought to combine the two."

"Oh!" Mandy's gaze swept the table as hot blood rushed to her face. "Sorry. I wasn't paying attention," she mumbled, then snatched up the pieces of good china and replaced them with the everyday stuff.

No, she couldn't imagine how things were going to get worse, but she was pretty sure they would.

A few minutes later they all sat down to dinner, her mother and father in their accustomed spots at the ends of the table and the rest of them arrayed in between. To her dismay, her mother directed Stephan to sit between Joshua's high chair and Stacy. At least she hadn't seated him next to Mandy. Stephan, of course, wore his perpetual suit and, she was pleased to see, an uncomfortable expression.

She sat down and automatically reached for

Joshua's hand on one side and her brother's on the other.

"We join hands while we say grace," her mother explained, and Stephan complied, though she could see he was clearly puzzled.

Her father gave a quick blessing, and the next few minutes were spent passing the various dishes around. Mandy noted that Stephan seemed uncertain how to proceed with that activity, fumbling with the bowls, clumsy about serving himself, hesitating before passing them on.

"It's serve yourself here," she explained as she cut up Josh's meat, potatoes and carrots for him. "The maid has the day off."

Across the table her grandmother paused with a bite of potato halfway to her mouth and arched an eyebrow, giving Mandy a silent reprimand.

"We're pretty informal around here," her father said, and she knew he'd caught his mother's look. "We help ourselves to food, including snacks. Anything you can find in the refrigerator is fair game. And we dress for comfort. Because this is the Lord's Day, the ladies are wearing skirts and we guys slacks, but we usually all wear shorts. Nothing wrong with what you've got on, of course. Very nice suit. But if you get too hot, feel free to dress a little more casually."

"I appreciate the suggestion. I'll have to obtain more appropriate clothing."

"Doesn't it get hot where you live?" Stacy asked.

"Not really. Eighty degrees is a scorcher for us."

"What's it like to live in a castle?"

"Actually, we live in the palace. The castle is pretty much a tourist attraction now. Most of the time it's quite chilly, actually, which probably explains why we always wear suits, to keep us warm. Your house is much nicer with all its windows and light.''

"How old is your palace?''

"The main portion was built sometime in the 1600s.''

"Wow! And I thought our house was old.''

"How old is your house?''

"New, compared to that!''

"Almost a hundred years,'' Mandy said, feeling the need to let him know that their family, too, had history and tradition. "Our great, great grandfather built it for his bride when she moved here from Atlanta.''

He gazed at her past Josh, who was happily shoving potatoes into his mouth with one hand and carrots with the other. "So your family isn't originally from here.''

She took one of Josh's hands, wiped it with her napkin and placed his spoon back in it. "You're in America now. Only the Native Americans are originally from here, and that's especially true in Texas. We're one of the oldest families in the area.'' Even as she said the words, she wished she could call them back. Why was she trying to compete with him on his terms? She couldn't, of course. What she needed to make him see was how important her family was, how much Josh needed them, not how socially acceptable they were.

Josh offered Stephan a bite of roast. Stephan looked at the boy then back to her, and his uncomfortable—verging on panicky—expression had returned.

"Joshua, Stephan already has some roast on his plate. That's your roast. You eat it.''

"'Kay!" His uncoordinated stabs at his mouth met with success on the second attempt.

Stephan lifted a hand to gesture around his own mouth. "He, uh, has food all over."

"Yes, he does. But there's no point in wiping it off until he's finished. He'll just get more of it all over."

"I see."

That was better, back into something she knew about and he didn't...though when she'd first brought Josh home, she'd had no idea how to care for a baby. She'd been almost as mystified as Stephan and had been totally dependent on her mother and grandmother to show her. Without her family, she would have been hopeless. However, she'd had lots of time to practice now, and Stephan had had none. Not to mention that she had lots of time to love the messy little urchin that Stephan saw only as a prince with food all over his face.

The rest of the meal proceeded without incident. Stephan cleaned his plate, folded his napkin and sat back with a sated expression on his face. "Excellent meal. The beef was quite tender, and your selection of spices enhanced the superb flavor. Our cook would love to have your recipe. Actually, I'd love for him to have it!"

Her mother smiled and blushed and promised to write it down for him before he left.

Dan leaned back, patted his stomach and beamed at his wife. "Everything Rita makes is wonderful. And wait till you try my mother's coconut cream pie." He pushed himself to his feet. "Is everybody ready to take our dishes into the kitchen so the ladies can clean up and we can have some of that pie?"

"You boys go on. We'll get the dishes tonight." Rita stood and began to gather the plates.

Dan kissed her on the cheek. "Thanks, sweetheart. Come on, guys, before she changes her mind."

Usually Mandy encouraged Josh to go with the guys while Stacy and her mother cleaned up the kitchen, but tonight she let him stay with her and even gave him pieces of silverware he proudly carried into the kitchen.

"I think it's going all right so far," her mother said, squeezing detergent into the sinkful of hot water.

"Very well, I'd say," her grandmother added. "He's a polite young man."

"Here!" Josh handed Mandy a spoon.

"Thank you, sweetheart." She gave the spoon to her mother to wash. "It's way too soon to tell about His Royal Highness in there."

Lynda brought in a stack of plates. "He seems nice. Not snobbish and stuck-up like you'd expect a prince to be. And he's a real hunk!"

"He sure is," Stacy agreed. "Can't you just see him at the ball?" She grabbed Lynda's hands and the two of them whirled around the kitchen in an exaggerated semblance of a waltz, then collapsed into giggles.

Mandy took out a clean dish towel and started to dry the glasses her mother was washing. "Will you two get a grip? It's bad enough my little sister's acting like a fruitcake. She's a teenager, but, Lynda, you're a married woman, about to become a mother!"

Both culprits giggled. "Like you haven't noticed how sexy he is," Lynda said.

"You all seem to be forgetting that this man is here to take Joshua away from us!"

The pair sobered. "He won't do that," Stacy said. "He's trying really hard to fit into the family. Now that he's getting to know all of us, he won't take Josh away. He'll probably just come back to visit, and maybe sometimes we can all go over there to visit, and when he's grown, Josh can decide how he wants to deal with this king thing." She knelt in front of the boy. "Hey, Josh! You want to be a prince?"

He ran to the door. "Pins! Pins!" The dog bounded up and sat, looking hopeful.

"Good for you, Josh," Mandy said. "You've got the right perspective on this royalty business."

Now if only she could keep the right perspective. Her family liked Stephan. In spite of herself, she liked him, too. He was making an effort to fit in. He wasn't the ogre she'd first imagined.

But he still posed a threat to her family, and even if he didn't, he was still a wealthy prince. Lawrence had never meant to hurt Alena, she was sure. It was simply part of the package. Riches and power brought heartache and pain under the best of circumstances. And having a rich, powerful prince staying under the same roof—a charming prince who was trying to make a favorable impression on everybody so he could steal her son—wasn't even close to being the best of circumstances. Pretty close to the worst, in fact.

Mandy sat on the front porch the next morning, sipping coffee and savoring the minutes just before dawn. The world was always totally still at first, frozen in time, then a single bird would awake and begin to sing, summoning hundreds of his buddies of every species, all soon warbling in an amazingly synchronized chorus, calling up the sun. From three houses down, Frederick Hunter's old rooster added his strident voice at periodic intervals.

When the door opened, she turned, expecting to see her grandmother, the other early riser in the family, who frequently joined her for this sunrise ceremony.

Yet somehow she wasn't surprised when Stephan stepped out onto the porch. Why shouldn't his intrusion into her life be complete?

"Good morning," he said. "Do you mind if I join you? This is my favorite time of the day."

That figured. "I see you found the coffee. Hope it isn't too strong. We like to start things off with a bang around here."

He sat in the chair next to her. This morning he had dispensed with the jacket and tie and wore only charcoal slacks with a long-sleeved white shirt, open at the throat, the cuffs unbuttoned and rolled up just enough to expose muscular forearms sprinkled with dark hairs. He somehow managed to look stiff and formal and deliciously sexy at the same time. "Actually, I brought some tea from home and made myself a cup. We don't drink a lot of coffee in my country."

She peered at the dark liquid in his cup. "That's tea?"

"It's what we call breakfast tea. A bit stronger than yours, I suppose. We like to start things off with a bang, too." He smiled, and the sun chose that exact moment to crest the horizon. Well, he was royalty after all. Even had the sun at his fingertips.

Mandy sat back in her chair and drew in a deep breath, snatching her attention from him to focus on this special moment of the day.

"Astonishing," he murmured. "There's a marvelous scent in the air, almost as if the sun brings with it all the fragrances of the lands it passed over during the night."

She jerked her gaze back toward him, uncomfortable, yet disgustingly thrilled that he'd shared the special moment with her. "You can smell it, too? I thought Nana and I were the only ones who could do that."

He took a couple of tentative breaths. "Yes, I smelled it. It's gone now, though."

"It only lasts a few seconds. You have to be here at just the right time to catch it. Is it the same in your country?"

He looked out across the yard, then back to her and smiled again, the expression a curious mixture of humor, arrogance and wistfulness. "I don't really know. The palace doesn't have a front porch."

She got up from her chair, fighting the ridiculous urge to feel sympathy for this man because his palace didn't have a front porch. "Well, I'd better go in and get breakfast started. The whole crew'll be up soon."

"You Americans don't do this sort of thing much, do you? Several generations living in the same house, I mean. Even your brother and his wife have another home."

She turned, perched on the rail and faced him. "No, this probably isn't the standard living arrangement. We have lots of room in our country, and we all want our own space, our privacy. I once thought that was what I wanted, but—" She shrugged. "I didn't. After my grandfather died and then Josh came along, I realized the importance of family, so I moved back here instead of staying in Dallas."

"I thought perhaps you were required to return home in order to adopt Joshua, since you're not married."

"It helped. The Taggarts really wanted somebody else to adopt Alena's baby. That way there'd never be anything to link the kid to them. I was single, just out of graduate school, had a lot of offers for jobs in Dallas but I hadn't accepted one, so coming back to a stable home helped my case. But that wasn't the main reason." She looked around her, at the sturdy, ancient live oaks that provided not only shade and shelter from the Texas sun, but a sense of stability in a world that changed continually and not always for the better. "I sat on this same porch and looked at those same trees when I was a little girl and then as a teenager and now as a woman. This is my home. It's where I belong."

"Do you journey to Dallas every day to work?"

"Oh, no. The offers I had were all for fast-track management positions. I'd have had to work long hours, weekends, travel a lot. I didn't want to do that once Josh came into my life. I'm a grade school teacher right here in Willoughby. One day I'll have Josh in my class." *If you don't take him away from me.*

"Your mother said you were doing volunteer work at the library when I came by Saturday morning."

"I have the summer off, so I try to help out a little in the community."

"Your father mentioned last night that he owns a hardware store and your brother works there."

Mandy knew her father was completely unpretentious, but she couldn't help but wonder if he had been trying to reassure Stephan about their status in life, that they were in a financial position to raise Josh. "That's right. My grandfather opened it when Dad was about Josh's age."

"Your mother, what sort of work does she do?"

"She's an old-fashioned homemaker," she said defensively, recalling his comments about his sister wanting to change the world and refusing to accept the traditional role of a woman in her country. "Raising the three of us and taking care of this big old house has kept her busy every day for thirty years. Now she takes care of Josh while I'm at work and if she has any spare time, she helps dad with the books at the store." She slid off the rail. "I hope you like big breakfasts with lots of cholesterol."

He smiled that devastating smile again. "When in Texas..."

Mandy was dropping biscuits into a pan when it suddenly dawned on her that with her father at work, her mother going with him to help him with some bookkeeping at the store, Nana going to a bridge club meeting and Stacy off to play tennis with friends, she'd be alone in the house with Josh and Stephan.

Just as she'd feared, things were getting worse by the minute.

After breakfast Mandy showered and dressed in shorts and a T-shirt, then got Josh dressed. They went downstairs, and Stephan emerged from the living room as they reached the entry hall.

"Stee!" Josh exclaimed happily and burst into an exuberant if incoherent spate of chattering. He finished and looked expectantly at Stephan who looked at Mandy, panic and bewilderment rearranging his normally composed features.

"That's great, sweetheart!" Mandy said, tousling Josh's soft hair. "Isn't it, Stephan?"

"Yes. Quite right, Josh."

"Why don't you go find Gamma and see what she's doing."

Josh scampered away, and Stephan blew out a long breath. "How do you understand him?"

"Practice. But I have to confess, I only get a word here and there. Best I could determine, he was telling you about taking a bath and a tiger coming in to steal his refrigerator."

Stephan looked even more bewildered. Much as she hated to admit it, he also looked even more appealing. "But that doesn't make sense," he said.

"Of course it doesn't. He's a little kid. He's just learning to talk. I don't even know for sure that's what he said. If he did, he could be making up stories again—which isn't the same as lying—or he could be talking about his dreams. At that age, dreams, television shows and reality get a little confused."

She allowed herself a small, tentative thrill of victory that Stephan was already realizing how ill equipped he was to raise a small child.

Of course, he undoubtedly had no intention of raising Joshua. That job would be passed to a succession of nannies.

"Do you think you could accompany me on a shopping trip?" Stephan asked, and her guard went up again.

"I'm not much of a shopper," she said warily. Was he going to try to bribe Josh with toys, bring home a carload, lavish him with everything in the stores the way Alena's parents had done for her?

"I understand. But I could use a little help selecting

appropriate clothing. I feel as if I'm still overdressed.''

She laughed at the understatement of his self-assessment and in relief that he wasn't planning a toy marathon. "You are a little overdressed. Okay, we can do that. I'm on my way to the grocery store, anyway.''

He smiled in a way that was almost boyish, and she could see the family resemblance to her son. "Very good! I've never been to a grocery store.''

"Never been to a grocery store? Oh, of course. Your servants would have done that.''

"The staff, yes. We don't have *servants*. My country isn't that backward. Everyone who works for us is quite well paid. We even have a pension plan.''

"The staff, the servants, it's still a million miles away from Willoughby. I'll get the grocery list, and we'll go.'' She started to leave, then turned back. "This is a small town. Gossip travels fast and I don't want Joshua's life disrupted by a horde of reporters descending on us. If we run into anybody I know— and we're bound to because I know pretty much the entire town—I'll introduce you as a relative who's visiting for a while. A shirttail relative from up north. That won't be a total lie since you are Josh's uncle, and the northern part will explain your accent. Not that you sound like you're from any part of this country, but people down here just think Yankees talk strangely. Any accent will work.''

He placed a hand over his flat midriff and looked down. "Shirttail relative? Must I do something different with my shirt?''

She laughed. "A shirttail relative is someone who's only distantly related, usually not even by blood, like your mother's second cousin's husband's nephew's wife's sister's oldest son.''

His eyes widened in astonishment, then he laughed, too. The sound was rich, round and deep and vibrated through her, warming and exciting her entire body, like that first cup of coffee in the morning, except with sexual overtones.

It made her feel really good…and that was bad. That worsening effect she'd noticed this morning was climbing the chart. Stephan hadn't even been here twenty-four hours, and already she was getting in over her head. She had to put a stop to this attraction before it went any further. She had to remember that he wasn't a shirttail relative nor was he just a good-looking man who set off fireworks in her body. He was a prince, a wealthy, titled foreigner who'd come to steal her son.

Maybe she ought to write it a hundred times, the way she made her students write things over and over so they'd always remember them. Maybe if she never looked into his eyes again or listened to him talk or laugh or got close to him or thought about him…

"I'll get that list for the grocery store and be right back," she mumbled, and darted from the room.

Even if she could avoid his physical presence—and she didn't see how she could—getting him out of her thoughts was going to be a lot tougher.

Chapter Four

"Extraordinary." Stephan pushed his shopping cart slowly down the aisle, apparently—amazingly—enthralled by the selection of items that spread out on all sides.

Josh, riding in Mandy's cart, kicked his short legs and said something that sounded remarkably close to "extraordinary." That's all she needed, for her son to start talking like a prince.

Mandy studied Stephan as closely as he studied the rows of merchandise. She'd decided on the new superstore up on the highway rather than the smaller, local clothing and grocery stores where she usually shopped. This place was enormous and impersonal, and she preferred the others. However, she'd chosen it partly to impress Stephan, to show him that his country had nothing on hers. She'd even sort of hoped the store might intimidate him—if that was possible—and emphasize to him that he was in her territory now. But mostly she'd chosen this place because they were less likely to be observed in a big store on the outskirts of town where people came from several surrounding areas than they were in the local stores where the clerks and the shoppers all called her by name and could remember when she'd lost her baby teeth.

To her surprise, Stephan did seem to be impressed, and so far she hadn't seen anybody she knew. Of course, they'd only been in the store a few minutes and between the handsome prince and her adorable son, everyone they'd passed had taken notice of them. With Stephan's regal air and good looks, he stood out. No chance of hiding him.

And maybe she shouldn't try. If he stayed at their house very long, someone was bound to notice and ask questions. Maybe the more open she was, the more likely people would be to accept her story that Stephan was a visiting relative.

Yeah, right. With that military-erect carriage, that accent and those elegant, tailored clothes? Not likely.

First she had to get him dressed properly. Camouflage clothing so he'd blend in with the peasants.

"This is the men's section." She indicated a table piled high with denim and khaki shorts. "I'm sure it's not the quality you're accustomed to, but there's no point in spending a lot of money on clothes you'll never wear again when you leave here."

Her words held a challenge that he would be leaving, and soon, but if he noticed he ignored it.

"Good point." He began to sort hesitantly through the items on the table, but almost immediately his uncertain movements stopped. His expression when he looked up at her was probably as close as he ever allowed himself to come to helplessness. "These sizes are most peculiar."

"Yes, well, they're in inches, not centimeters or whatever measurement they use in your country. You're just going to have to try on a few. I'd say you're probably somewhere around a thirty-four, maybe a thirty-six." She blushed as she realized what she'd just admitted—that she'd been studying him closely enough to estimate his waist size. "The dressing room's over there," she added hurriedly, in an attempt to divert his attention from her inadvertent admission.

A flicker of something passed through or behind his glacial eyes, then disappeared before she could identify it. He looked in the direction she pointed.

Gamely, he gathered up several pairs of shorts and headed toward the dressing room only to be stopped by the woman guarding the entrance.

"How many you got there, cowboy?"

"Excuse me?"

"How many garments?"

Mandy moved up beside him. "She wants to know the number of items you're taking in."

"Why does she wish to know that?"

"So they can be sure you bring out the same number."

His brow furrowed, then, as understanding dawned, his shoulders squared and his nostrils flared indignantly. Obviously the Prince of Castile wasn't accustomed to being accused of potential shoplifting.

"He's from up north," Mandy explained quickly before he could say anything. "You know how different folks are up there." She counted the items, and the woman, bored and disinterested—thank goodness—handed her a plastic tag which she passed to Stephan. "Here you go...cowboy." She couldn't resist adding the last. Although the woman had used it as a generic title, the idea that anyone would call Prince Stephan Reynard a cowboy brought a smile to her lips.

"Cow!" Josh exclaimed, banging his hands happily on the metal bar of the shopping cart. "Cow! Mooooooo!"

Stephan returned her smile and inclined his head in a mock bow. "Perhaps I should purchase some boots and a hat, also."

"Not with the shorts."

"Right." He went into the dressing room, as square a peg as she'd ever seen. Totally out of place in her world. Okay, they'd just shared a cute moment, a *cowboy* moment, and that morning at dawn they'd shared a beautiful moment. But they still lived in two different worlds.

"Cow!" Josh repeated.

"Not really." She spoke as much to herself as to him, as if warning herself not to get confused as to Stephan's identity.

"Cute kid," the woman said. "Looks like his dad."

For a moment Mandy wondered how she knew about Lawrence, then realized she meant Stephan. She groaned silently. That was all she needed, for people to think Stephan was the father of her child. There had been enough talk when she'd returned to town with a *supposedly adopted* child and no father. Even *accidentally* leaving the adoption papers in the copy machine at the library hadn't completely silenced the small-town gossip.

This downhill slide they were on was picking up momentum.

As they shopped for shorts, shirts and casual shoes, Stephan maintained his stiff upper lip, but she could see him becoming frustrated with the difference in sizes, the narrow range of selections, and store policies like the clothes-counting routine. By the time they moved into the grocery section—successfully skirting the toys—Mandy was feeling a little guilty for enjoying that frustration so much. But only a little. The less control he had over the situation, the more she'd have and the better the chance he'd give up and go home…soon…without Josh.

And without tempting her any further with these crazy thoughts about his waist size or the sprinkle of hairs on his forearm or the way his voice resonated around some chord inside her breast or the silly *moments* they seemed to be sharing, but weren't, of course. This was worse than the time she had a crush on her fifth-grade teacher.

Far worse.

Only children dared to fantasize about princes. Not that she'd been fantasizing about him. Not really. Okay, maybe a stray thought or two for the sprinkle of hairs on his forearm and the sensuous way his lips moved when he spoke and on the rare occasions when he smiled. But that wasn't the same thing as fantasizing.

She concentrated on selecting fresh vegetables for a salad.

"Appa!" Josh demanded, reaching for the bright red display.

"They do look quite appealing, don't they, Joshua?'' Stephan examined the fruit with as much curiosity as a child.

"Why don't you pick out half a dozen of those for eating, and I'll get some of the MacIntosh for Nana to make a pie.''

With surprising zest, Stephan chose the largest, reddest apples he could find, then the biggest pineapple and cantaloupe and went on to fill her cart with a wide variety of items as they made their way through the store. She calculated the amount of cash she'd brought for grocery shopping. It probably wouldn't be enough. Well, she'd write a check. Stephan would not, of course, have the slightest concept of a budget, of not buying everything a person wanted.

"Spam?'' he read, picking up the rectangular tin. "Isn't that something to do with the Internet?''

"Spam!'' Josh echoed with the delight of discovering a new word. "Spam! Spam! Spam!''

She took the can from Stephan and shook her head in amazement. "Most people in this town have never heard of spamming on the Internet, but they know exactly what this product is. Of course you'd be the exact opposite. This is food. It came before the Internet. It's been around longer than you or I.''

"It's aged? Like wine?''

"No, I don't mean this particular can. I mean they've been making this product for years.''

"I see.'' He retrieved the can from her, his fingers brushing hers in the process. No, it was more than a brush. It came close to qualifying as a touch. It was enough to start the heat rising in her. Enough to make her look away and refuse to meet his eyes, refuse to let him see what she was feeling or to let herself see if he felt that same heat.

This really was ridiculous. Lusting after a prince while surrounded by Vienna sausages, sardines and Spam.

He bent his dark head and studied the label.

"Oh, no!" she protested. "Don't read the ingredients."

"Why not? I want to know what's in it."

"You probably don't. It's sort of like a ham, only all ground up with spices added then pressed back together."

"How peculiar. Why would they grind it up and then press it back together?"

She stared at him for a moment, uncertain if he was serious or teasing. He had the ability to look solemn and flippant at the same time, as well as incredibly sophisticated and naive. Dangerous combinations. Irresistible combinations. *Almost* irresistible.

"Because hams aren't square and wouldn't fit into the tin," she finally answered.

"I suppose that makes sense." He carefully situated the Spam in her cart.

The dessert section of the frozen food department got his complete attention.

"Here's an apple pie. We could get this, and your grandmother wouldn't have to make one." He opened the glass door and took out the box.

"That's not quite the same thing. Nana makes her pies from scratch."

"She scratches the fruit?" He looked up from studying the instructions, mystified.

"She prepares everything from the basic ingredients," Mandy explained. "She doesn't buy it already made."

"Are these pies good?"

"Well, yes. Not as good as Nana's, but they're okay."

"Is it a lot of trouble to cook from, uh, scratch?"

"Some."

"Then why doesn't your grandmother buy it like this? It says here all you have to do is put it in the oven and bake for an hour. Wouldn't that be easier?"

"My grandmother enjoys cooking for her family. It's part of our tradition, and you know how important traditions are."

He studied her and then the pie. "Yes," he said. "I know quite well the importance of traditions."

"I'm sure the royal chef does all your cooking from scratch."

He considered that a moment. "Probably. But that's his job. He gets paid for doing it, and he has a staff to help him."

"Nana does it for love. That's her payment."

"I see." She didn't think he did, but she let it drop.

He put the apple pie into the cart, then selected a pecan. "They had this flavor at the hotel. It's quite nice." He reached into the freezer case again and selected a cherry.

"Do you have a *thing* for pies?" she asked.

"I enjoy dessert," he said.

Josh applauded and chattered about *dert*.

"He enjoys dessert, too," Mandy said, as if that fact wasn't obvious. She eyed the frozen treats. "But Nana's going to get her feelings hurt if you bring those in the house. She takes pride in her baking."

"If she gets her feelings hurt, I'll apologize and immediately dispose of the offending pies."

"Fine." It wasn't fine at all, but surely her grandmother would understand that Stephan, coming from a different culture, was bound to make an occasional faux pas. And she didn't care if her grandmother got upset with him. The whole family was already upset with him, and it was only likely to get worse the longer he was around.

When they finally made their way to the checkout line, Mandy's cart was overflowing with frozen pizzas, picante sauce, chocolate milk, three flavors of ice cream, the pies, a couple of frozen cakes, two packages of cookies and other assorted items that had captured Stephan's interest, including tape bubble gum and gummy candies—gummy worms, gummy bears, gummy hearts, gummy spiders.

Of course Josh had gone bonkers when they reached the candy section. He always did, but he knew he could have only one thing. However, in spite of her admonitions, Stephan had loaded the cart with everything Josh pointed to until she finally persuaded him to stop.

They already had enough sugar to send them all into a diabetic coma, she told him through gritted teeth. Sugar was not good for children or other living creatures. But he gave her that distant look of his, oblivious to her words or secure in the knowledge that such a rule, like most rules, didn't apply to a prince.

Maybe they didn't.

As the clerk scanned the groceries and Josh slobbered around a gummy worm, Stephan stood behind her, a solid presence, touching her with his nearness. The scent of the same soap everyone in the family used drifted to her, recognizable yet different, imbued with Stephan's essence of masculinity, royalty, sophistication and this new element of naiveté she'd just glimpsed. It was a heady, alluring combination.

"Mandy!"

She jumped at the sound of her name. Carol West, a waitress at the Willoughby Grill, stood in line at the next checkout counter. If Carol wasn't the biggest gossip in town, she was certainly a finalist for the title.

"Hi, Carol!" Mandy made a futile effort to sound enthusiastic rather than terrified.

Carol smiled and batted her eyelashes so hard that Mandy expected bits of mascara to fly off them and land on the bald head of the man standing in front of Carol. "I've been trying to get your attention forever, but I guess your mind was somewhere else." She shifted her eyes slightly, looking meaningfully behind Mandy, at Stephan.

Mandy turned to include him in the conversation. "Carol, this is Stephan, my cousin from up north." Better stick with first names only, just in case. "He's visiting for a few days."

"I didn't know you had any relatives up north."

"Oh, sure. A whole branch. Stephan is my grandfather's brother's wife's nephew. Great nephew."

"Oh, a shirttail relative."

One corner of Stephan's mouth quirked upward in something that almost resembled a smile. He dipped his head in a slight bow. "That's correct. A shirttail cowboy. It's an honor to meet you, Carol."

Carol smiled and twisted a strand of blond hair around one red-tipped finger. "You have got the cutest accent, Steve. Whereabouts up north are you from?"

"New York," Mandy said, her hand moving to take his arm in a proprietary gesture, even as her mind ordered her hand to stop the ridiculous action. Not bad enough she'd lost control of her hormones. Now her body parts were taking off on their own, too.

"How long are you staying, Steve?"

"Not long," Mandy replied.

"If you're still here Saturday, I'm sure Mandy will bring you to the big Fourth of July barbecue down at the lake. Afterward a bunch of us are going up to Dallas to the Rawhide and Lace Club for a little boot-scooting. They've got a great band. Do you two-step?" The last was delivered in a coy voice that suggested the question could mean more than a dance.

Unfortunately Stephan probably would still be there on Saturday, and now that he'd been spotted, she'd have to take him to the barbecue, but she was going to nip any other plans in the bud. "Carol, he's a Yankee. You know they don't two-step or do the Cotton-Eyed Joe or even wear boots to scoot."

"But, Cousin Mandy," Stephan protested, "I've been taking lessons."

She looked up at him, aghast. He still wore his dignified, staid expression except for that one little corner of his mouth that kept twitching upward. He was obviously enjoying her discomfort as much as— or more than—she'd enjoyed his earlier. His fingers closed over hers where she still held his arm, and her heartbeat immediately went into a country waltz rhythm. She couldn't have looked away from him if she'd tried. Not that she particularly wanted to escape the delicious feeling of his hand on hers, his body beside hers, his breath warm on her cheek. "Wouldn't you like to see how well I can two-step…Cousin Mandy?"

Oh, yeah. She definitely would. Two-step, three-step, sidestep, as long as he touched her, held her in his arms.

His eyes were smoky and warm—no, hot—giving a double entendre to his words, and she realized with a jolt of sizzling pleasure that the attraction she felt for him was mutual. Those glimpses she'd had of banked fires beneath the civilized veneer had been real and, wonder of wonders, those fires were springing to life because of her.

"Is this all together?"

Mandy whirled at the sound of the new voice. The woman ringing up their purchases indicated the clothing Stephan had piled on the counter.

"Yes," he said before she could say *no*.

He let go of her hand and reached inside his pocket to withdraw a wallet.

She stiffened. "I'm buying the groceries."

"Please allow me. I did, after all, select most of them."

Short of making an embarrassing scene in the store and giving Carol more fodder for gossip, Mandy could think of no response other than "Thank you," spoken through gritted teeth. At this rate she was going to wear the enamel off her teeth long before Stephan left town.

As they exited from the store, Carol waved and called after them. "Bye now! See y'all Saturday."

Stephan waved back. "Right. See y'all Saturday." Spoken in his formal accent, the familiar phrase sounded ridiculous. He was as bad as Josh, repeating every new word he heard. If she hadn't been so angry, she might have found it endearing.

Mandy didn't speak until they were inside the family van with the doors closed and Josh was securely fastened in his car seat holding another gummy worm. He'd have the disgusting candy all over the car and himself, but she wanted to be sure he was quiet for a few minutes.

She turned to Stephan and spoke coldly. "I'll write you a check for the cost of the groceries. You don't need to buy food for us. We're quite capable of buying our own. You're our guest, and guests don't provide their own food."

He sighed and ran a hand through his immaculate hair, leaving it still immaculate. "In my country, being a guest does not mean taking advantage of your host. A guest who arrives without gifts is considered a very rude guest. Gifts are based on the giver's ability and desire to give, not the needs of the recipient. I shall be happy to have my father send you a jeweled music box or a painting by one of the masters or an emerald necklace to match your eyes. In the alternative, you can permit me to purchase groceries and perhaps to take your family out to dinner a few times. The choice is yours."

It took Mandy a second to catch her breath. The business about the emerald necklace could have been a compliment, but he'd delivered it in his usual emotionless voice and continued right on with his next statement, so probably it wasn't.

"We're not in your country now," she said. "We're in mine, and we'll play by my rules."

He lifted an eyebrow and smiled. "Is that any way to treat a guest? I thought you Texans were proud of your reputation for hospitality."

She clenched her teeth and could almost feel the enamel eroding. "It always comes down to money, doesn't it?"

"No, it does not. It comes down to courtesy."

She had no retaliation for that.

She gave the key a vicious twist in the ignition and stomped on the gas as the engine roared to life.

No matter what he said, money *was* the issue. It always was. Money gave power and with it inevitably came the need to change things...usually not for the better.

To give him credit, Stephan probably wasn't doing it consciously. He'd always had wealth, always had the power that went with wealth as well as the power that went with royalty. She thought of the confidence in his eyes as he'd looked down at her and placed his hand over hers, then asked if she'd like to see how well he could two-step.

To her chagrin, she had to admit that she was as drawn to Stephan as she had been so many years ago to Alena's shiny new toys and expensive clothes. Those things had changed Alena's life and hers.

That desire to have what she didn't need, what wasn't good for her, had taken her to Dallas to get a degree that would land her a well paid, glamorous job. And while she'd been gone, her grandfather had died. She'd lost a part of the thing that really mattered, her true wealth, her home and family.

And she'd lost her best friend because of wealth and royalty.

Now Stephan was here to change her life again, to take all that was left of Alena—her son, Mandy's son—and raise him in that same unhappy world that had wrecked two lives already.

Mandy drove as fast as she dared, anxious to get home to her family, to have them around her the way it had always been, safe and unchanged except for Gramps. She needed to hold on even more tightly to what remained of that world, keep it the same…keep Stephan out.

Chapter Five

Stephan studied his reflection in the dresser mirror of the Crawfords' guest room. He had to admit the new clothes were cooler and more comfortable. In some of the warmer countries he'd visited, like Italy and Greece, he'd been tempted to join the tourists in garments suitable to the climate, but had always felt he should maintain his image as a member of the royal family of Castile. Now in Willoughby, Texas, he was a *cowboy*, a *shirttail cousin* named Steve...and he didn't even have a shirttail.

He grinned at his image. Cowboy Steve could wear shorts and knit shirts with impunity.

Feeling oddly exhilarated and free, he left the room and went downstairs.

He didn't see Mandy or Joshua, but, mingled with the music of birds and insects that drifted through the open windows, he could hear the boy laughing and shouting and the dog barking. *Prince*. That's what they called the dog. At first he'd thought it an insult, but now he wasn't so sure. They did treat that dog like royalty.

He followed the sounds to the front porch, stepped outside then stood for a moment, watching. Mandy tossed something across the yard, then Joshua and the dog ran after it while Mandy cheered them on.

Mandy wore a pair of denim shorts similar to his, wore them without a trace of awareness of the incredible way she looked in them. Every male in the store that morning, including him, had been unable to take his eyes off her long, slim legs and rounded derriere. The white T-shirt she wore, imprinted with the lone star flag of Texas and the slogan, "Don't mess with Texas" hugged the curve of her breasts in a demure yet tantalizing way.

She'd pulled her mass of curls back into a ponytail with a few stray curls wisping about her cheeks, a cooler, more practical way of wearing it than down. He liked her hair falling about her shoulders in splendid disarray, but this style emphasized the clean lines of her face. She was an attractive woman now. With that bone structure, she'd age into graceful beauty.

As she leaned forward, clapped her hands and shouted for boy or dog…he wasn't sure which…to "get that bone!" Mandy had a regal dignity and presence even though she played this game, as she did everything, with passion.

Joshua, on the other hand, didn't even come close to looking like a prince as he hurled himself to the grass and tried to wrest the bone away from the dog.

After a few moments the dog graciously relinquished the coveted toy, and Joshua, his smile wide, face dirty, clothes stained with grass, took it back to Mandy. Stephan could just imagine the queen's face if she could see her grandson, the future heir to the throne, right now.

Uncomfortable with the involuntary smile that image conjured up, Stephan moved across the porch and down the steps.

Josh spotted him, dropped the bone and charged over, arms wide. "Stee!"

"He wants you to pick him up," Mandy said, and her tone of voice told him she wasn't entirely pleased with that. "Lean over, open your arms and pick him up," she ordered when he didn't move. She might not have royal lineage, but she could certainly issue orders with the authority of a queen.

Feeling a bit self-conscious, Stephan followed her directions. Joshua clasped him about the neck, and Stephan awkwardly lifted the boy, who planted a loud, moist kiss on his cheek, then leaned back and began babbling in that foreign language. His small body was solid in Stephan's arms, and he smelled of grass and dirt and childhood.

His eyes were Lawrence's.

Memories flooded over Stephan, long-ago memories of his sister, Schahara, and him, sneaking out of their rooms and going to big brother Lawrence's to huddle together in one bed during the cold, dark nights, memories of the three of them comforting each other when Nanny Angela had left, then Nanny Francis and Nanny Catherine. After that, he couldn't remember the nannies' names. Lawrence had passed on the wisdom of his superior years to his younger siblings…don't learn their first names. Don't get attached. It's easier when they go if you don't learn their first names.

Even in those early days, Lawrence had assumed

the role of leader by dint of being two years older.
As Stephan gazed into the eyes so like Lawrence's—
except his brother's had never sparkled the way
Joshua's did—Stephan realized he was now the older
one. He had the responsibility of taking care of this
boy, of seeing that everything was done right, and that
responsibility encompassed a lot more than avoiding
the names of nannies. This boy's entire future rested
in his hands, and he had to get it right.

How had this simple expedition become so complicated?

"You guys ready to go in for a little lunch? Come
to Mommy, big boy."

Speaking of complications...

Mandy held her arms toward Joshua, and he clam-
bered to go to her. Stephan relinquished him. She'd
told him to pick up the boy because that was what
Joshua wanted, but then she'd wanted him back. For
a moment her gaze held his, and he realized she was
as confused as he.

They both wanted what was best for Lawrence's
son. The problem arose from their diametrically op-
posed ideas of what that best might be.

One of the problems, anyway.

The other arose from the way he felt every time
this pushy, stubborn, passionate woman got close to
him.

The sun glinted off her fiery hair, and he couldn't
resist this time. He touched one of the tendrils that
curled about her face and found it was indeed
hot...though he couldn't be sure if it came from the
color or from the sun or from his own hand.

Her eyes widened in surprise, then the pupils
slowly dilated. Her lips relaxed as though she could

read his mind and know how much he wanted to kiss those lips, as though she anticipated that kiss.

They were standing in her front yard in bright sunlight, and she held Joshua in her arms. Even if circumstances were different, if the boy wasn't in the picture, if their paths were parallel instead of briefly crossing, this was neither the time nor the place for a kiss.

For Mandy Crawford and Stephan Reynard, there would never be a time or a place. He had his duties, and getting involved with an American wasn't one of them. Getting involved with anyone, for that matter, would be foolish. Lawrence had forgotten that and caused pain to himself and several other people. Stephan wouldn't make that same mistake.

Nevertheless, his hand cupped her cheek and his mouth moved toward hers, touched the silky smoothness of her lips, clung for an instant of delight, of rushing blood and surging libido and promises of wonders unexplored, then, reluctantly, mustering every ounce of strength he could find, he moved back into the emptiness of the summer air.

She blinked, whirled away from him and climbed the steps to the porch.

"I'll make Spam sandwiches," she said, and only the slight breathlessness in her voice betrayed that anything had happened.

But it had.

It certainly had.

The kiss had lasted the space of a heartbeat, yet now everything was changed. The electricity that flowed between them had been acknowledged. Now, no matter how much they might act as if it wasn't there, as if they didn't notice, each would know that for a lie.

There was nowhere to go from here, yet rather than satisfying his longing for her, the kiss had been petrol on glowing embers.

He wanted more.

And he couldn't have it.

Even if the issue of Joshua hadn't stood in the way of anything personal between them, their very lives stood in the way. He was a prince with duties to fulfill that went far beyond his own small needs. He couldn't let his emotions cloud his judgment the way Lawrence had done. All his life he'd seen and been taught the destructive elements of emotions.

He couldn't have more of Mandy, no matter how much either of them might want it.

She was like dessert. He could never get enough of the sugary treats, knew they weren't good for him and knew he should never even start. But he couldn't resist the tempting sweets, no matter how fleeting their flavor on his tongue. From the time he was a baby, he'd been taught self-control, and he'd learned it well...except for desserts—and now, Mandy Crawford.

He thought of Lawrence's long-ago advice and wondered if it would have been better if he'd never learned her first name. Certainly it would have been better if he'd never known her lips. But he knew both.

If only he could go back in time and undo the kiss.

Except he wouldn't do that even if he could. Not for all the treasure at the bottom of the ocean. Not even to avoid all the complications he could see arising.

* * *

Stacy dried the last glass, set it in the cabinet and turned on the water to rinse the silverware Mandy had just washed. "It was nice of Stephan to get those pies so Nana doesn't have to bake for a while."

Mandy plunged her hands into the hot, soapy water, snatched up a plate and scrubbed vigorously. "Nana's pecan pie is much better than the one we had tonight." Though that wasn't really the point. She resented Stephan's inroads into her family. He didn't fit into their world, he was the antithesis of everything she and her family valued. That fact was becoming increasingly obvious. Yet, at the same time, it didn't seem to matter. At least to the others. It certainly mattered to her.

"True," Stacy said, "but I'll bet Nana liked this one more."

"Why on earth would you say that?"

"Because she didn't have to make it, silly."

Mandy frowned at her sister. "Nana enjoys cooking for us. She's always said that."

Stacy shrugged. "I know. But she sure seemed pleased when she found all that frozen stuff in the refrigerator."

Mandy watched the bubbles swirl as she withdrew a bowl from the soapy water. "Oh? I must have been outside with Josh when that happened." She'd spent most of the afternoon and evening avoiding Stephan after that brief but unforgettable kiss. However, she hadn't been able to avoid recalling the moment...over and over, again and again.

Dinner had been almost painful with the longing to meet his gaze and search those inscrutable eyes for the counterpart of the desire he'd roused in her. But she didn't dare. She didn't want to know if the kiss had been as powerful for him as it was for her. That kiss had given her a comprehension of why Alena had been unable to stay away from Lawrence even when she knew there was no hope for them. Though Mandy was only too well aware that the gulf that separated Stephan and her was even wider than the one that had separated Lawrence and Alena, she couldn't seem to stop thinking about the feel of Stephan's lips on hers.

"I guess you were off somewhere," Stacy said. "Stephan asked her if she minded about all the prepared food, and Nana said it was the best present she'd received since the foot massager."

"She really likes that foot massager."

"Yeah."

"That's strange. Remember last year when I tried to help her by making dessert for a while? She insisted she wanted to do it herself."

"Well, sure, but your desserts were so bad, Prince threatened to run away from home if we made him eat the leftovers."

Mandy laughed and flicked her sister with water. "Okay, okay! Point taken!"

She washed a few more dishes, then paused and looked out the window at the long shadows of evening. "Nana's not sick, is she?"

"I don't think so. Why would you think that?"

Mandy shrugged and resumed her task of washing. "I thought maybe she didn't feel like baking anymore."

"You don't have to be sick to get tired of doing one thing and want to do another."

"What does she want to do?"

"How should I know? Travel, maybe. See the world. Date."

Mandy looked at her younger sister in shock. "Date? Nana? Did she say that?"

"No, she didn't say it. But Gramps has been gone for three years. It could happen. You think she just wants to hang around here and bake cookies for us?"

That was, Mandy realized with a touch of embarrassment at her own selfishness, exactly what she'd thought, that Nana would be there to make chocolate chip cookies and brownies for Josh just the way she'd done for Mandy, Stacy and Darryl when they were growing up.

"Of course Nana has a right to a life of her own," she said. "She can bake or not bake, date or not date. It's just kind of a shock, that's all. Different."

A difference brought about by Stephan. Whatever he did, whether it involved something as big as Josh or as inconsequential as Nana's pie-baking habit, took on a frightening aura. The sensation of her world spiraling out of control had begun when her grandfather died and had only, over the last year, begun to slow down. When she walked in to see Stephan in their house three days ago, that terrifying sensation had returned full force. Now every minor difference he made to their routine seemed somehow an inroad to taking Josh from her...to taking from her the life she'd only recently started to trust again.

Not that the kiss they'd shared had been minor. That had been pretty major, actually.

Resolutely she shoved the image from her mind. It happened. It was over. She had to stop thinking about it.

"Hey, I have a great idea," Stacy said. "Let's get paper plates and plastic spoons and then we won't have to wash dishes!"

"Right. And if we get paper clothes, we won't have to do laundry."

"That's a good idea."

Mandy rolled her eyes. "First time you get rained on, your clothes'll melt."

Stacy giggled. "Then I'll bet Kyle Forester would notice me."

Mandy regarded her little sister affectionately. For the first time it registered that Stacy wasn't so "little" anymore. At sixteen, she was almost as tall as Mandy, and her body already had the womanly curves that would, indeed, get her noticed by the male of the species if her clothing suddenly dissolved in the rain.

Stacy was growing up, just as she and Darryl had done. It was the natural order of things, yet tonight it only added to the feeling that everything in her life was whirling around at a rapidly accelerating speed, getting farther and farther out of her grasp.

Mandy continued to banter with her sister, but her thoughts wandered to the front porch where Stephan would be sitting with the rest of her family, enjoying the relative cool of the evening. She found herself hurrying with the dishwashing so she could get out there with them. To protect her family from him, of course, not just to see him again.

When the dishes were done, Mandy dried her hands and headed outside, but Stacy lagged behind. "I'll be out in a minute," she said. "I just want to call Megan about our homework assignments."

More likely Stacy wanted to talk to her friend about Kyle Forester, Mandy thought. *Changes.* But she smiled. "See you in a little while."

Mandy moved on to the screen door, then paused for a moment to savor the scene. Her mother and grandmother sat on one end of the porch in a glider, while Stephan, her father, Lynda and Darryl lounged in lawn chairs on either side. Josh and Prince were, of course, running around the yard in some chaotic game only they understood.

The long summer evening was still light but with softer hues than the brilliance of day. The elegant live oak, graceful magnolia and stately cottonwood added further dimensions to the sun's last lazy efforts. The scent of honeysuckle drifted in on a gentle breeze that barely rustled the leaves.

If dawn with its new beginnings and promises was her favorite time of the day, evening was a close second, when all the work was done and the whole family could relax together.

She opened the door and went out to join them.

"We had the sonogram today," Lynda said, patting her slightly rounded tummy. Even in the gathering dusk, Mandy could see that her face was radiant.

"Yeah, and the doctor thinks it may be triplets," Darryl said, winking.

"Oh, he does not!" Lynda swatted her husband playfully. "You stop that!"

Mandy unfolded another chair and joined them, avoiding even a glance in Stephan's direction. "Can you tell if it's a boy or a girl yet?" she asked.

"Not yet, but he or she is really active! Josh is going to have some competition for the title of most hyperactive kid in the family." Lynda stopped suddenly, bit her lower lip and looked at Stephan then quickly away.

Everyone was silent as the darkness of evening seemed to move in faster and the still air hung heavy and oppressive with the unspoken question of whether Josh would continue to be a part of the family.

"Guess what, Mandy-girl," her father said, his voice determinedly upbeat as if to ward off the gloom, "Stephan and I are discussing ways to remodel the kitchen and put in a dishwasher."

"And a built-in microwave," her mother added. "It'll be great to get that thing off the cabinet and free up some space."

Two desirable changes. But if Stephan was involved, they somehow became scary changes.

She turned to face him. He wore his new attire of a white knit shirt, cutoffs and casual shoes and managed to look like an incredibly sexy prince on a throne as he sat on their porch in an aluminum folding chair with one loose strap that dangled to the floor. "Is kitchen remodeling part of your princely training?" she asked.

"In a way, yes. I found it fascinating to study how the different styles of architecture have evolved in different countries through the centuries, the blending of practicality and beauty, the concessions to climate and surroundings. Take your own house, built in a predominantly hot climate at a time when air-conditioning was unheard of. You have high ceilings to let the heat rise, with carved molding to relieve the expanse of wall. Beauty and concession to the climate. You have windows on opposite sides to encourage a cross breeze. You have several bedrooms because large, extended families were common in those days."

"Are you saying our house is outdated?" she snapped.

"Of course it is," Nana said smoothly, her words

and tone a gentle reprimand that Mandy was not minding her company manners. "What else can you expect from a home that's almost a hundred years old?"

Stephan smiled. "Yes, your house is outdated, but please don't take offense. Remember, I live in a house that's a couple of centuries older than yours. Keeping it livable is an ongoing task."

"But you have a staff for that," Mandy said.

"Yes, we do, a fairly large staff that works full-time on keeping the palace livable."

"And you're not involved in the actual work." *So stay out of the renovations of my home...of my life!*

"I plan to be involved. I have several ideas."

"I'm more than happy to let you try out some of those ideas right here," Dan Crawford said. "This old place could sure use some renovations. Now that Darryl's taking over a lot of the work at the store, I'll have more time for things like that. Central air would make sleeping a lot nicer in July and August."

"Installing central air wouldn't be that difficult," Stephan assured him. "One way to go would be to drop the ceiling and then..."

Mandy didn't hear the rest over the winds that roared through her ears. She got up and crossed to where Josh now sat quietly digging in the dirt with Prince looking on.

She sat beside them and drew Josh into her lap. He was hot and sweaty and dirty and she loved him fiercely. "Tired, big boy?"

"Uh-uh," he denied, shaking his head, then leaning it against her, eyes already half-closed.

Mandy rocked him gently.

"I haven't done this in a while," said Nana. Mandy

looked up to see her preparing to sink to the earth beside her. "Good grief, I sound like a bowl of cereal when you pour on the milk."

Mandy smiled at Nana's summation of the creaking and popping of her joints.

"If I had my druthers, I'd druther be young." She adjusted her slacks, then patted Mandy's hand and smoothed Josh's hair. "It's going to be all right, you know. Stephan's not a monster. He's not going to steal Josh from us. We'll find some sort of compromise."

"I don't want a compromise. I want everything to stay the same." To her surprise and consternation, Mandy felt tears start in her eyes. She blinked them back, grateful for the darkness so no one could see. "I sound like a spoiled brat, don't I? I know he's just trying to do his duty, and I know I ought to be pleased that he's offering to help us with the house, that something good could come of this nightmare. I know I'm overreacting. It's just that...remember when I was a little girl, I'd whine about the fact that Alena didn't have to do dishes because they had a dishwasher, Alena's family had air-conditioning in the summer and heat in the winter, their plumbing never growled like some wild animal about to attack us, the refrigerator never had to be defrosted...and nobody was happy."

Nana wrapped her arm about Mandy's shoulders and gave her a hug. "But we'll still be happy when we have all those things. That won't make us stop loving each other."

"I know. It's just that since *he* came here, everything's changing so fast. I guess if I had my choice,

I'd go back in time, not forward. I'd go back to when we had Gramps and Alena.''

Nana laughed softly. "And I wouldn't sound like a bowl of cereal when I sat down. That would be wonderful. I still miss your granddad every minute of every day. But then we wouldn't have Lynda and the new baby...and we wouldn't have Josh.''

Mandy smiled. "I'm greedy. I want it all.''

"We're leaving!" She turned to see Lynda and Darryl walking toward her. "Night, Josh," Lynda said, and leaned down to kiss his head. "Oh, I can barely do that! It won't be long before I won't be able to bend over at all!''

Darryl hugged his wife. "I know. I'll have to polish your toenails for you. Just promise you won't tell our kid when he gets old enough to ask. See you tomorrow, folks.'' He waved, and they went to their car.

Mandy tried to rise, but discovered one foot had gone to sleep. Between that and the weight of her son, she fell back to the ground. Stephan appeared from the darkness and took Josh from her.

"Thank you, Stephan," Nana said, as if she knew Mandy was about to make an absurd, impolite protest.

"Yes, thank you," she echoed, standing up and reminding herself that he was helping. That's all.

"Stee," Josh murmured drowsily and burrowed against Stephan's chest. The action tore at Mandy's heart. Of course she wanted Josh to bond with his uncle, yet at the same time she found his acceptance of Stephan terrifying. Would he be willing to go with this man, if not now, in later years? Would his acceptance of Stephan include the glamour and wealth of Stephan's lifestyle?

"Good night," Nana said, and moved off toward the porch.

Mandy reached to take her son from Stephan, but stumbled on her still-prickly foot. He caught her arm, steadying her.

The night was warm but his touch was warmer, heating through the skin and all the way inside, flowing like a river of liquid fire through her veins, into her breast, through her lungs, making it hard to breathe.

"Thank you," she managed to whisper. "Again."

He continued to hold her...with his hand and with his gaze. His eyes were as dark as the sky overhead and just as fathomless. In the stillness of that gaze, a cricket's song burst onto the night air with a beauty and clarity she'd never heard before. The scent of honeysuckle she'd noticed earlier had combined with Stephan's sophisticated, masculine scent and become a tantalizing essence that promised delights beyond her imagination. She could taste his lips as if they were again pressed to hers. Her entire being yearned toward those lips, toward him.

His hand moved from her arm to her hair and pushed it back from her face.

She knew she ought to run as far and as fast as she could from this temptation. Stephan was as seductive as those shiny new toys Alena used to get all the time...and just as dangerous to her soul. She was every bit as hypnotized by the allure of something fascinating that she couldn't have as she had been in the long-ago days of childhood.

Josh shifted and mumbled something in his sleep, and the spell was shattered...and Mandy was relieved and disappointed.

Stephan dropped his hand from her cheek.

She reached for Josh, and Stephan surrendered him.

Her son's breath was warm on her neck as she carried him to the house, but Stephan's gaze burned all the way down her back as surely as if he continued to touch her. She walked without wavering, her head high.

Her fear wasn't simply that Stephan would try to steal Josh. Nana was right. He wasn't a monster. Her fear was that Stephan could offer him so many "things"…money, power, a title…that the boy would leave of his own accord. She hated the idea of her son becoming involved to any extent whatsoever with that lifestyle. That lure had drawn her from her home and family to Dallas. It had taken her grandfather's death and Alena's tragedy to make her see the treasure she had at home. She didn't want Josh to make the same mistake.

She didn't want herself to make that same mistake again.

Chapter Six

The week passed in a blur, and Saturday came far too soon. Mandy wasn't ready to face the town at the big barbecue with Stephan by her side pretending to be a relative. He hadn't kissed her again since that moment in the front yard, but after that, every glance, every accidental touch they exchanged had been a caress. She knew only too well that they'd kissed in his dreams just as they had in hers. Too many times she'd turned to see him looking at her and, just before he'd glanced away, she'd seen the fire in his normally glacial eyes. Too many times the incidental touches had lingered an instant too long…and not nearly long enough.

He wasn't up yet when she and her father left just before dawn to drive to the lake to get things started. A group of men from the town, including her father, would begin cooking the meat, and she was on the committee to set up tables, lay out game sites, drape the bandstand with red, white and blue bunting, see that the microphone worked and otherwise prepare for the big party.

This was the first dawn she'd greeted without Stephan since he'd been there. Not that they had any kind of planned meeting or had intentionally shared it. They were both early risers and came out to view the same event at the same time, which wasn't the same thing as doing it together.

Nevertheless, she felt oddly out of kilter without him.

Lucy Frasier, already there when they arrived at the lake, hailed her with a hearty, "Is your cousin Steve gonna be here?"

"Yes," she answered, stretching her lips into a smile. "He's looking forward to it!"

"We're all looking forward to meeting him. Carol says he has the cutest accent even if he is a Yankee."

Carol had obviously spread the word.

As they worked, the sun rose higher in the sky. The day would be bright and perfect, though it would soon be hot. But the park around the small lake had plenty of trees for shade, and the residents of Willoughby were accustomed to heat. They'd have lots of cold soft drinks and iced tea as well as chilled watermelons and dozens of freezers of homemade ice cream to cool them off, and the kids would splash in the shallow end of the lake. Beyond that, they'd be having too much fun to worry about a little sweat.

As noon approached, all the efforts were falling into place. The smell of barbecued ribs, chickens and briskets filled the air and made Mandy's stomach growl with a reminder that the only breakfast she'd had was a chocolate-frosted doughnut from the selection someone had brought.

She stapled a red-and-white-checked plastic cover onto one of the weathered picnic tables and tried to focus on that activity or on her growling stomach…anything to distract her from constantly looking up to see if the rest of her family and Stephan had arrived yet.

"Mandy, honey, would you come help me get this flag up?" Susan Bingham asked. "This silly rope is hung or something."

Mandy went over to the tall flag pole and gave the rope pulley a hard yank. "It was just stuck." The flag rose smoothly to the top where a breeze caught and unfurled it for a moment of magnificence.

"Does your cousin celebrate the Fourth?" Susan asked.

"What do you mean?" Had they somehow found out about Stephan's true identity?

"Him being a Yankee, and all. I didn't know if they celebrate the same holidays we do."

Mandy blinked in astonishment, but all she said was, "Yes. The Yankees celebrate Independence Day. Thanksgiving and Christmas, too."

She'd planned to brief Stephan on the history of the day, but had gone into the living room last night to hear her father and him discussing the Revolutionary War and how it compared to Castile's own battle for freedom from England centuries before.

Stephan continued to be totally out of place in Willoughby, Texas, and yet somehow he continued to fit in more and more.

She was stapling on the last plastic tablecloth when she heard a familiar voice.

"Mama, Mama, Mama!"

"Woof! Woof!"

Two familiar voices.

She looked up to see Josh charging toward her as fast as his little legs would carry him and Prince bounding along beside him.

She reached down, scooped up her son and whirled him in a circle. "How's my boy?"

"Picnic!" he exclaimed.

"Hey! You learned a new word! Are we having a picnic today?"

"Picnic!" He pointed a chubby finger, and she looked to see Stephan coming toward them.

A *picnic* was about the last thing she'd call Stephan Reynard, but she supposed the term had some relevance since he was carrying an ice chest as he crossed the grass toward her.

Then it hit her. "Did you teach him to say that?" she asked as Stephan approached and set his burden on the table.

"It's not really necessary to teach him to say anything. He repeats everything he hears. He's a very bright child."

The pride and affection on his normally expressionless face as he looked at Josh both pleased and frightened her. As a mother, however, she couldn't help but join him in that pride.

"Yes," she agreed. "He's pretty sharp. Aren't you, kiddo?"

Laughing, Josh squirmed down from her arms, grabbed Prince around the neck and babbled something then looked up at her expectantly. "Yes, I see you brought Prince. Good idea. Every picnic should have a prince." *Or three.*

Her mother, Stacy and Nana joined them carrying a huge chocolate cake, a large bowl of mustard potato salad and a giant fruit salad with poppy seed dressing, the dishes they brought every year.

"Food looks great! I'll take the cake over to the dessert table."

"And I'll get the ice cream freezer from the van," Stephan offered.

Mandy was relieved when Josh followed her instead of Stephan. Of course, she was carrying a chocolate cake. That could be considered undue influence.

Fanny Walker strode across the grass bringing her infamous angel food cake with lemon glaze. Someday somebody was going to point out to her that most angel food cakes were higher than two inches.

But it wasn't going to be Mandy.

"Hi, Fanny! Come set your delicious cake right here next to Nana's devil's food cake. That kind of sounds appropriate, doesn't it?"

"It does, for a fact. Look at this boy! You're just growing like a weed!" The older woman stooped to Josh's level. "Come give your old Aunt Fanny a hug!"

Josh looked up to Mandy, his eyes wide.

With her stark black hair done up on her head in intricate curls, bright red lipstick that didn't stay strictly within the lines, large white teeth and scent of mothballs, Fanny probably didn't resemble most of the people Josh was accustomed to hugging. However, when Mandy nodded at him, Josh reluctantly put his arms about her neck, then quickly released her.

"Oh, you are just the sweetest thing!"

"Stee-eeve!"

Mandy looked up at the sound of another familiar woman's voice and saw Stephan lugging the ice cream freezer with a panicky look on his face as Carol tripped over to him.

The Annual Willoughby Fourth of July Picnic and Barbecue was in full swing.

Any thoughts Mandy had had of salvaging the day went straight down the tube when the crowd was finally gathered and Mayor Ron Cantrell stepped up to the microphone, welcomed everybody and asked them all to recite the Pledge of Allegiance to the American flag. She hadn't thought about briefing Stephan on that.

All in all, he didn't do too badly, though she had to grab his right hand and lay it over his heart, and his lip sync was always a few beats behind. She could see Susan, standing a few feet away, watching him closely. Maybe Mandy should have just let the woman think Yankees didn't celebrate the Fourth of July.

When the pledge ended and the mayor began his speech, everyone sank to the ground in anticipation of the long-winded rhetoric. On the opposite side of the bandstand, Mandy saw Susan lean over and whisper in Paula's ear. Paula's eyes and mouth rounded in shock, and she looked in their direction. And Mandy knew the town would have something new to gossip about...not only Cousin Steve, the Yankee who looked far too much like Mandy's "adopted" son, but that same Cousin Steve's ignorance concerning American traditions. She could only hope that didn't lead them to pry too deeply into the life of the man who sat on the grass beside her and held her son in his lap.

This morning she'd thought that things couldn't get any worse. They could, they would and they did almost immediately. Stephan's bare leg brushed hers as he resettled Josh on his lap. Brushed hers but didn't move away, remained lightly touching hers, the soft hair tickling her skin, the heat and electrical impulses from his body teasing that same skin.

She knew he couldn't move because of the other people crowded around. She also knew he didn't move because he didn't want to and because she didn't want him to.

Oh, yeah. Things were rolling downhill like a runaway train.

Stephan was in culture shock from the food. Meat cooked over an open fire until it was black-crusted, then covered with a sweet, spicy sauce so hot it burned the eater's lips, beans cooked until they were mushy in a similar but not-so-hot sauce, tangy potato salad, tart fruit salad, three-bean salad, jalapeño pepper halves stuffed with cheese, every kind of dessert imaginable including something called buttermilk chess pie that, in spite of its peculiar name, Stephan was sure must be the ambrosia referred to in the legends of Greek gods.

He sat between Josh and Nana, across from Mandy and the rest of her family on a wooden bench that left him with splinters in his bare legs if he moved too quickly. The bench was attached to a plastic-covered wooden table in the shade of a tree.

The strange food was incredible, and he'd eaten far too much. As he'd proceeded through the line at the table where all the dishes were spread out, he'd been besieged with urgings of, "You have to try my beans, Steve!" or "my green bean casserole" or "my mother's recipe for cheese grits."

He calculated there must be several hundred people at this picnic and most of them had brought food. He'd been introduced to at least half of them and, even with his training in remembering names of party guests, he had no hope of remembering most of them. But it didn't seem to matter. They sat at tables identical to the one where he sat, as well as on blankets and quilts, chattered happily as they ate, and clapped him on the back when they passed. It was complete chaos, but the energy, vitality and friendliness of the people was contagious.

He drank the rest of the iced tea in his plastic glass. He was actually beginning to like the odd beverage. It was quite refreshing after all those spicy dishes.

"Plenty more ribs over there," Dan said.

"Thank you, but I've eaten too much already. It was very good."

"You'll be hungry again by the time we serve the ice cream," Mandy predicted. "At least, you'd better be, or you'll hurt a bunch of feelings, judging from the way everybody's been clambering to get you to eat their food."

"'Scream?'" Josh asked, looking around at the mention of one of his favorite things.

"Not for a while. You've already eaten enough for three little boys. Are you finished with your cake?"

Josh crammed one more bite into his mouth even as he nodded vigorously.

"Then we'd better get you cleaned up before you go play. Chocolate frosting, barbecue sauce and strawberries are a bad enough mess. We don't need you adding dirt and grass to the mixture. It could become volatile, and then what would we do with an exploding boy?'' She climbed out of her seat to come around to his side of the table.

Stephan looked at Joshua who, as if sensing his gaze, looked up, a huge grin on his stained face. He did, indeed, have all the elements Mandy had mentioned spread over his features in a colorful array. He even had some sauce in his hair.

Again Stephan was struck with the amazing resemblance to Lawrence except... "Lawrence was never that messy in his life.''

"Yeah, well, Josh isn't Lawrence,'' Mandy snapped, lifting her son.

Stephan realized he'd spoken the words aloud. "I didn't mean—'' He wasn't sure what he had meant. "I'll go with you.''

She met his gaze, hers a challenge. "You don't need to do that.''

"Yes, I do.''

He'd been at the Crawfords' house for almost a week. It had been the most comfortable and the most uncomfortable week of his life. He'd learned a lot, yet was much more in limbo and confused than when he'd arrived at their door that first day. There was a week remaining of their agreed-upon time period, but he and Mandy needed to talk now. Though they'd exchanged pleasantries, especially in the early mornings, they'd avoided anything of import. When she was around, she muddled up his thought processes along with his libido, and that didn't seem likely to change. This was as good a time as any to clear up a few things.

He followed her to a public drinking fountain where she wet a washcloth and proceeded to scrub most of the food from Joshua's face, hair, neck, hands, arms and legs.

"I didn't mean that in a bad way," he said. "About Lawrence. It was just an observation. Sometimes Joshua reminds me so much of his father."

"Faer?" the boy asked curiously, tilting his face upward to peer at Stephan.

"Josh, go see Grandma. Mama'll be there in a minute."

"Okay! Bye!" He dashed across the grass toward the table where the rest of the Crawford family still sat.

"Don't say things like that in front of him," Mandy admonished. "He's not deaf and he's not stupid. He understands every word you say."

"Lawrence was his father and he needs to know that."

A couple of laughing teenagers came over to the fountain and bent to get a drink. Mandy turned and walked away, leading him to a more secluded spot down on the bank of the lake. She stepped carefully over the exposed roots of a tree that formed a vee-shaped area. In the point of the vee, she leaned against the trunk and stared out over the water.

"It hasn't been two weeks," she said.

"I know. I just thought we should discuss some things."

"Like what?" She turned her gaze toward him. Her eyes mirrored the leaves above them and the grass below. Or those elements of nature mirrored her eyes. Her hair, stirred by her movement and by a stray breeze, was like autumn leaves falling about her shoulders. Her lush lips pressed tightly together, and she folded her arms over her rounded breasts. She was the personification of this beautiful, colorful, stubborn land, and he was totally intrigued with both of them.

Suddenly he found himself at a loss for words, his vocabulary diminished to the size of Joshua's. Mandy had that effect on him.

The tree roots formed an effective barrier to keep him from getting close to her without making a deliberate effort. That was good…even though it didn't feel all that good.

He cleared his throat.

"Your barbecue is nice. The people are very friendly and everyone seems to be having fun."

"They are."

"They treat me like royalty, though no one knows. Your family has treated me with kindness since I arrived here, though you have every reason to shun me."

"Southern hospitality with a dash of Texas barbecue. It's what we do to our enemies. Lull them into a false sense of security, then feed them barbecue that burns their mouth so badly, they can't talk again."

She smiled and he laughed softly. "This town, your family, none of it is anything like I expected. When I spoke a few minutes ago about the difference between Joshua and Lawrence, I didn't mean to speak aloud." He shrugged. "Or maybe I did. Maybe I wanted to talk about some things that have been on my mind. Lawrence was two years the elder so I wasn't around to know him when he was Joshua's age, but sometimes I see my brother in the boy. His eyes, especially. Except Lawrence's eyes were always old even when he was still a child. He had a lot of responsibility."

"I don't want that for Josh. I want him to be a

little boy without a care in the world for as long as possible. Were you and Lawrence ever young? Did you ever play and have fun?''

Stephan leaned against the tree trunk beside her and stared out over the still water. It was easier to talk if he didn't have to look into those all-knowing eyes. ''We had playtime, and many of our lessons were presented in the form of games. If it was less than what other children had, we didn't know. You don't miss what you don't know about.''

''You missed having real parents.''

He considered her comment and wasn't sure how to answer. A cicada overhead broke into its raspy song. People laughed and shouted only a few feet away while he and Mandy stood wrapped in a cocoon of shade.

''Lawrence told Alena,'' she continued when he said nothing, ''about being passed from one nanny to another, how the three of you only had each other and he tried to take care of you.''

''He did. When it stormed, Schahara would come to my room, and the two of us would go to Lawrence's where we'd all huddle together until morning.'' In the midst of the summer heat, the memory brought back the sensation of the coldness of the palace and the small spot of warmth the three of them had created.

''Do you miss him?''

''His death was tragic and unnecessary. It was a great loss.''

''I didn't ask you to deliver a eulogy. I asked you if you miss your brother. You're in America now and you're not royalty over here. You're my shirttail relative named Steve, and it's okay for Steve to have feelings.''

He hesitated, unsure how to answer truthfully and still maintain his dignity, stay true to his training, the stiff-upper-lip philosophy. This woman demanded nothing less than the truth from him. "Terribly," he finally admitted. "I miss him terribly."

"Me, too. I miss Alena, I mean. They were an awful lot alike, you know, your brother and my friend. Neither had much of a family life. For a little while they had each other, but they never really stood a chance.''

"No, they didn't. Lawrence was very wrong to get involved with her. He knew what his duty was. We were taught from the cradle that we had responsibilities, that an entire country was depending on us. As you're so fond of saying over here, it's a dirty job but somebody's got to do it.''

"You don't want the job, do you? Lawrence didn't, either.''

"It's not a question of wanting or not wanting." He ran a hand through his hair in frustration at this beautiful, stubborn…and far too insightful…woman. "I'm sure Alena didn't want a child under the circumstances, but if she'd lived, she'd have loved him and cared for him no matter how much he interfered with her plans. You did the same thing. Because of your love for your friend, you took her child to raise and changed your plans completely.''

"No. I added Josh to my plans. I already knew I wanted to come home to my family. Josh gave me the guts to throw away everything else and do what I wanted. By raising Josh the way I was raised, I can make up in a small way to Alena for all she missed.

And to Lawrence. Even though I blame him for what happened, I feel sorry for him.''

"Tell me,'' he said, biting off the last word as his voice started to crack. These emotions, once unleashed, were dangerous creatures, difficult to banish to the dungeons again.

"Tell you what?''

"About them. Lawrence and Alena.''

She moved away from the tree to stand in front of him, arms folded across her chest, forcing him to look at her. "Why?''

"I need to know.''

"Why?''

For several moments they gazed at each other in silence, and once again he knew that nothing less than the truth would satisfy this woman. He cleared his throat.

"He was my brother. I need to have this last piece of him.'' It was the truth, though he couldn't tell her how desperately he needed that last piece...how passionately. It was hard enough to admit to the bald fact of his need.

Her gaze searched his face for a few more seconds, then she nodded, apparently satisfied with his explanation. He suspected she knew all the things he couldn't put into words.

"They met in a poetry class. When they first started going out, I liked Lawrence. He made Alena happy.''

"And she made him happy.''

"Yes, she made him happy. I wish you could have seen them together. They were like two little kids at the circus, both of them amazed it was happening to them. I think he told her the truth fairly early on, but she didn't tell me. She told me what he said about his parents and his brother and sister. She just edited out the part that he was a prince. For that entire year, they were together constantly and happy constantly. And then he left."

"To go to New York," Stephan said. "He had a rigid schedule to follow."

"Yes, to go to New York. Alena was devastated, and I hated Lawrence. I didn't see why he'd leave if he loved her so much. A few months later Alena admitted to me that she was pregnant."

"Lawrence could have married her," Stephan said. "The king would have been furious and there would have been many problems, but he could have. Why did he choose not to if he loved her so much?" As he asked the question, he realized this was what he needed to know. The brother he'd grown up with, while devoted to the kingdom, aware of his duties, would have felt some duty to his unborn child and the mother of that child, yet he'd left her.

"Because Alena loved Lawrence, she didn't want him to have to make that choice and she didn't want her baby to grow up the way Lawrence did. So she didn't tell him."

"She didn't tell him?" Stephan repeated incredulously.

"No, she didn't tell him. That's how badly she didn't want her baby to be a prince. She didn't even tell me until I figured it out and asked. I was furious with Lawrence. That's when she told me the truth about him. She was afraid if he found out, he'd do something noble and it would cause all kinds of problems for him…as well as for their child."

She dipped her head and bit her lip, then looked up again, defiantly. "She'd tried to tell her parents early on, and they said they would cut her off financially unless she got an abortion. After that debacle, she hid it from everybody. When she admitted it to me, she made me swear that I wouldn't tell anyone. After her parents cut her off, she didn't have money for prenatal care, so she didn't go. I gave her money and made her go to the doctor, but the problems had already started. When she went into labor, I got scared and broke my promise. I searched her room, found Lawrence's and her parents' phone numbers and called them both. Lawrence came immediately. Her parents didn't come until it was obvious Alena was in trouble.''

She turned away and went back to lean against the tree. "You know the rest. When Alena realized she was dying, she and Lawrence conspired to keep their son a secret. By the time Alena's worthless parents got there, they had it all worked out. I would raise Josh, and Lawrence would go home and do his duty.'' She spat out the last word as though it left a foul taste in her mouth.

Stephan stood in silence for some time, looking out over the lake. Rather than giving him a feeling of closure, rather than returning this last piece of his brother to him, the story told him how little he'd really known about Lawrence.

"He knew the rules,'' he finally said. His voice sounded weary to his own ears, and he wondered if he was talking about Lawrence or about himself. "He knew the consequences of breaking them.''

He looked at Mandy and found her looking at him. Her eyes searched his face as if she, too, knew he was talking about himself as well as Lawrence, warning her that, no matter how tempting she was, he couldn't become involved with her...for her sake as well as his.

"Do you think he regretted it?" she asked quietly. "Would he have undone it if he could? Like the way I wish I could undo the time I left home, when I went to Dallas and got an MBA so I could make lots of money and see the world? I wanted what Alena had, the glittery things that money can buy. But while I was trying to get those *things,* my grandfather died, and suddenly having a lot of *stuff* didn't matter. I lost part of the only world that really matters. If I could invent a time machine, I'd go back and never leave home. I'd go to school in Dallas so I could be with Alena, but I'd still live at home. I'd appreciate and treasure what I had before I lost it. I grant you, letting himself get involved with Alena caused all sorts of problems, but do you think, if he could, that Lawrence would go back in time and do things differently?"

Stephan thought about it for a long moment. "I don't know. Maybe. He loved his country. I think he would have been content as our ruler. If he could go back in time, forego those few moments of *the grand passion* and all the months of pain afterward so that he and Alena would both be alive, yes, I think he would."

You don't miss what you know nothing about, he reminded himself. If his brother had never loved Alena, he'd never have lost her. And Stephan wouldn't have lost his brother, nor would he be here on a mission to bring back Lawrence's son, a mission that became more confusing every day.

On the other hand, he'd never have met Mandy Crawford, never have known the intimacy of being included in her family.

And he wouldn't have to face the pain of being split apart from that intimacy, never again experiencing the pleasure of watching dawn arrive with Mandy sitting beside him or kissing her lips so briefly as they stood in her front yard with the warm breezes caressing them, or touching her every chance he could, even though those touches had to appear accidental.

You don't miss what you know nothing about.

Never learn the first name of your nanny because she's only temporary and it doesn't hurt so much when she goes if she doesn't have a name.

"But you don't have a time machine," he said, "so we all have to live with our choices and the choices of those around us." Live with them and get through them as safely as possible.

"There you are!" Carol stepped around the tree roots and came to stand beside Stephan, then looked from him to Mandy and back again. "I hope I'm not interrupting anything."

"No," Mandy assured her. "We were just talking. Family stuff."

"They're about to start the balloon toss. You don't want to miss that!" Carol linked her arm through Stephan's. "Do you already have a partner for the three-legged race? I'd plumb love to do that one with you. Me and Ricky Trussell took first place last year but he's down in his back."

Stephan looked frantically over his shoulder at Mandy for help. He had no idea what a three-legged race was, but he was pretty sure he didn't want to run it with Carol. "I'm a bit down in my back, also," he protested.

"That accent is just so cute! Say something else."

Mandy stepped up and took his other arm. "Sorry,

but Stephan promised to run the three-legged race with Stacy. It's an old family tradition.''

He gave Mandy a grateful look. She released his arm and they walked back up to join the crowd.

You don't miss what you know nothing about.

But he knew about her touch on his arm, and he missed it.

Chapter Seven

Mandy pasted a smile onto her face as she followed Stephan and Carol to rejoin the party. Stephan had as much as told her...warned her...not to become involved with him. Of course she'd had no intention of doing so, but she supposed a little reminder never hurt.

Except it did.

In spite of knowing better, she was attracted to him. His touch, his glance, set her on fire, started her hormones and her adrenaline to gushing. And, she realized, she'd sort of become accustomed to having him around. If nothing else, his presence beside her on the porch while they watched the dawn had become a piece of her life...a pleasant piece.

She knew he was a prince, a man of wealth and power with his duties laid out before him. She knew he was all the things Lawrence had been and more. Lawrence had wanted to break away from his duties; he just couldn't. Stephan didn't even want to. Stephan was comfortable in Castile. He was comfortable being cold and aloof. She'd just made him uncomfortable by forcing him to confront his feelings about his brother.

She knew that wealth and power brought unhappiness. They'd killed her best friend. She'd lost her grandfather while pursuing those things.

And Stephan personified wealth and power.

She wished she'd let him continue wearing his suit and tie. It would have been easier for her to remember who he was if he looked the part. Instead, in his khaki shorts and white knit shirt, he almost looked like an ordinary guy. Well, an ordinary, regal, drop-dead-gorgeous guy. One who could turn boyish with no warning, who got a panicked expression on his face at the thought of running the three-legged race with Carol Price.

Two lines were forming for the balloon toss, and Mandy, Stephan and Carol joined them. She didn't feel much like playing games, but she didn't feel much like feeling sorry for herself, either, and that was just what she was likely to do if she didn't take steps to avoid it.

"Mandy!"

She looked halfway down one line and spotted Stacy, Josh and Prince. "Excuse us, Carol, we need to go help Stacy with Josh."

They moved down to join Stacy. She had both hands on Josh's shoulders but released him and turned halfway to include the teenage boy who stood next to her. "Kyle, this is my sister, Mandy, Josh's mom, and this is our, uh, cousin from, uh, New York, Stephan." Her face turned bright red as she spoke. Stacy didn't handle lying well. Thank goodness.

But she wasn't blushing just from the white lies she'd had to tell. This must be the Kyle that Stacy wanted to notice her if all her clothes dissolved in the rain. Stacy had always had a lot of friends, male and female. She'd even had a few casual dates, but this one seemed different. The look on her face was different, more that of a woman than a girl. Her baby sister, Mandy realized, was bridging the gap between child and adult.

Mandy had a sudden, overpowering urge to scream at her to be careful, to guard her heart, to consider long and hard before she began this move, to hang on to childhood and her family as long as she could.

Of course she said none of those things. She smiled at the blushing couple and extended her hand. "Nice to meet you, Kyle." He took it tentatively.

Stephan did the same, then Mandy explained the rules of the balloon toss to Stephan. "They fill the balloons with water, then toss them back and forth from side to side, and you try to catch it without breaking it."

He looked a little dubious.

"It's fun!" Stacy assured him.

"What happens if you break it?" he asked.

Stacy giggled. "You lose. And you get wet."

"And if you don't break it?"

"You stay dry."

"That doesn't seem so hard."

Mandy and Stacy exchanged a smile.

"Ba-oon!" Josh exclaimed, pointing down the line. A red balloon had begun its journey.

With each person who caught it, the balloon stretched and became more misshapen until it burst in the fifth person's hands. The crowd as well as the other players laughed, applauded and booed good-naturedly.

"Well," Stephan said, "that's that. Now what do we do?"

"Oh, no!" Mandy corrected gleefully. "You're not off the hook so easily. The next person gets a new balloon until we reach the end of the row. Then the team with the fewest wet people wins."

"I see." He looked uncertain, but stood his ground. Mandy smiled as she pictured his ancestors a couple of hundred years ago, dressed for battle, worried they might never see another dawn, but standing erect and ready to do the right thing in just that stance.

As the third balloon, a blue one, reached the person standing next to Mandy, she positioned Josh in front of her. "Okay, kiddo, get ready. Get those hands up. We've got to catch it next time!"

The young boy on the other side tossed the already-misshapen balloon to them, and Mandy, bending low over Josh, successfully made her catch, letting him grab the sagging end, He squealed in delight while Prince wagged his tail and barked.

With a great deal of juggling, Mandy lobbed the stretched-out balloon across to the opposite line.

Josh scooted in front of Stephan. "Do 'gain!"

To her surprise the balloon actually made it back to them...and Stephan, legs braced as if for battle and forehead creased in intense concentration, caught it without breaking it. But as it sagged between his hands and Josh reached for that part, Prince suddenly decided to join the game. The dog grabbed the balloon...with his teeth.

It exploded, splashing all three princes with water. Mandy stooped to Josh's level to be sure he was all right. His eyes were wide with shock, and he puckered up to cry, but then heard the laughter, applause and shouting and decided to clap his hands and laugh instead. That brought more applause from the crowd.

"I think we'd better take our little group out of the running," Mandy said. "Josh and Prince enjoyed that far too much. No balloon will be safe on our team again."

They backed away and stood watching from the sidelines.

"That was enjoyable," Stephan said, but he sounded a little unsure.

"Was it?" Mandy asked, barely able to restrain her laughter.

He thought for a moment and looked down at his soaked shorts. "Yes," he finally said and smiled. "Actually, it was rather fun. And I certainly feel cooler now."

He had a beautiful smile. It was the first time she'd really seen him perform the action with his entire face. Even his glacial eyes were warm like the summer sky overhead. His skin glowed with a sheen of perspiration and the glare of bright sunlight. He looked less and less like a prince, and it was all Mandy could do to hang on to the knowledge that he was, to avoid being sucked into the depths of those eyes and that smile.

The balloon toss ended with Mandy's side the loser by a substantial number of wet shorts, and the crowd started milling over to another area. Mandy took Josh's hand to lead him.

"What's this next one called?" Stephan asked. "Is this the three-legged race?"

"No, this is the father-son race. The father or big

brother or some male relative carries the kid on his shoulders and the first one across the finish line wins.''

"What does he win?''

"First place.''

"I see.''

She punched him lightly on the shoulder. "Everybody who enters is a winner because they have fun!''

"Ah! More of this elusive fun thing!''

Tom Anton and his son, Matt, a boy Josh's age, walked up beside them.

Josh stopped, looked at the other child who looked back at him. Josh touched the boy's face with one finger, and the boy returned the gesture.

Prince ran over to greet the new arrival, and both children laughed.

Tom smiled. "Hi, Mandy.''

"Hello, Tom. Where's Nancy?''

"She's around somewhere. Sent me off to do the race with Matt while she takes it easy in the shade with a cold soft drink.''

Mandy had known Tom and Nancy since grade school, and Matt and Josh played together in the church nursery. It was only natural he'd come up and say hello. She shouldn't feel paranoid, but she couldn't help it. Was Tom merely being friendly, or did he want to find out who this strange man was? Was everybody speculating as to his identity, or was she being totally paranoid?

"Tom, this is my distant cousin, Stephan, from out of town. He's visiting for a few days.'' She didn't like lying to her friends, but saw no other choice.

"Glad to meet you, Steve.'' With no trace of suspicion on his face, Tom extended his hand to Stephan, and Mandy relaxed. "You going to take Josh on this race?"

"No, I think not."

"Okay. See you later!" He reached down and lifted his son onto his shoulders as they arrived at the trail where white chalk marks designated the beginning as well as the end of the race. The participants would run to a point a hundred yards out, circle a tree and come back the same route. Meeting the obstacle course of slower runners on the return trip added an extra element of difficulty to the event.

Clasping and unclasping one extended hand, Josh reached for his friend, Matt, looked up to his mother and chattered, his small features anxious. "No, sweetie, Tom can't carry both of you! You're too big. You're such a big boy."

But Josh was unconsoled. He gazed up at Mandy with a pleading look, lifted his arms to her and babbled something that ended with "...ike Matt!" *Carry me like Matt,* she interpreted.

Mandy crouched to his level. "I can't carry you in this race. This is for little boys and their—" She hesitated and bit her lip. The subject of daddies hadn't come up yet. It probably would before too many more years, but this was no time to start. "This is for little boys and big boys, but Mommy's a big girl. She can't run in this race. It's against the rules."

To her surprise, Stephan reached down and lifted the child then placed him on his shoulders. Josh bounced excitedly and held on to Stephan's ears.

"You said other male relatives. I assume that includes uncles, cowboys and shirttail relatives named Steve, all of which I qualify for."

He's a prince, a wealthy, powerful prince from an-

other country, who has no place in my world and will only bring both of us unhappiness, she chanted over and over to herself as the two of them lined up in the midst of all the fathers and sons. But right now he'd made her very happy by making her son happy. She bit her lip in a vain attempt to still the confusion.

The race began, and Stephan and Josh were among the front runners. Stephan could have probably made better time if Josh hadn't been gleefully banging on his head. Stephan, however, seemed to be taking it all in stride and passed her with a wide grin and a wink.

The Prince of Castile winked at her.

"Sure can see the family resemblance." Mandy turned to see Carol standing beside her with a sly look on her face. "Oh, but Joshua's adopted, isn't he?"

"Yes, he is."

Well, that sure took care of that brief burst of happiness. If Carol suspected something wasn't quite right, she'd keep digging until she found out exactly what it was, not to mention spreading any and all lurid rumors she could come up with along the way.

For the first time since Mandy had moved back home, she couldn't bear to think about the future. No matter what Stephan decided to do about Josh, it would totally disrupt the plans she'd made for his life. And now the old rumors about his birth would start again. She saw no possible way to keep secret his status as heir to the throne. Once that came out, everything would change. He could no longer be a carefree little boy who loved to eat cake and ice cream and play with his dog. He'd be a member of royalty, and people would expect him to act differently. They'd treat him differently.

The crowd began to cheer as the front-runners of the father-son race loped by, heading for the finish line. Stephan was among them with Josh still waving his arms and laughing. Mandy jumped and cheered with everyone else. Only because of Josh, of course.

As he and Stephan crossed the finish line first, Mandy shrieked and applauded wildly, then pushed her way through the crowd to get to them.

Stephan was laughing along with Josh, who still sat atop his shoulders while everyone congratulated them.

And Mandy knew she'd lied when she told herself she was cheering only because of Josh. She was thrilled that Stephan had won. She was thrilled to see him happy, an emotion she wasn't sure he'd ever felt before. And she was thrilled that it had been something in her world that had made him happy.

His gaze met hers, and his excitement vibrated in waves across the summer air. She threw herself into his arms, hugging him while reaching up to Josh at the same time, sharing the thrill of winning. Something nagged at the back of her mind, something about this man causing potential problems with Josh, something about not getting so close to this man, but right now she couldn't remember exactly what any of those somethings were.

Though the sun was on its downward swing, Mandy thought the light seemed brighter as the picnic continued with more games and cold drinks. Prince went to sit with Nana in the shade of a tree on a slight rise near the deep end of the lake where the breezes were more frequent and cooler.

Mandy, Stephan and Josh moved with the crowd,

and she was forced into tantalizing proximity to Stephan by the push of the people around them. Actually, Stephan didn't make any effort to move away from her even when the crowd thinned at times.

He was, she thought, being an extraordinarily good sport in a situation she was sure he'd never experienced or even conceived of before. He didn't even seem to mind when someone jostled him and he spilled tea all over the front of his white knit shirt. If he attended any more picnics, she'd have to tell him that a better color choice would be beige or green or maybe something close to the amber shade of tea.

Of course, it was a moot point since he was leaving in a week and there weren't any more picnics scheduled between now and then. Back in Castile he'd return to his white-shirt, dark-suit and conservative-tie persona.

When it was time for the three-legged race, Stephan watched the preparations with apparent interest while he finished off another glass of iced tea. He'd certainly taken to the beverage after his initial reaction.

"You told Carol your sister and I would do this event together," he said, "but there Stacy is, getting her leg tied to Kyle's."

Mandy looked in the direction he indicated. The insipid grins on the faces of both Stacy and Kyle told her they didn't really care whether they won the race or not, as long as they got to move down the path together. Her sister looked happy, as did Kyle. Sixteen years old. It was the time for first loves. Still, Mandy felt a small ache as she watched the couple, a wistful ache for the world around her that seemed to be changing much too fast.

"You and I will have to do this together," she heard Stephan continue.

Have her bare leg tied to Stephan's bare leg? Run along the path with his body pressed against hers? Have the same insipid grin on her face that Stacy had? Her body thought that was a terrific idea, but her mind had better sense.

"I have to take care of Josh. Anyway, when I told Carol that you and Stacy were doing the race, it was just to get her off your case. You don't have to do the race at all."

"I understand you were improvising, but I believe I see Carol coming this way. Do you think I can convince her that my back is down like her partner from last year?"

A vision of Carol bouncing along the race route with her shapely leg tied to Stephan's and her other shapely assets bouncing along at the same pace filled Mandy with a strangely proprietary feeling.

Stephan was her guest and he shouldn't have to be tied to anyone he didn't want to be tied to. This was a simple case of Texas courtesy.

"Go line up," she said, "and I'll take Josh to stay with Nana, then be right back."

Nana was pleased to watch Josh for a while, and the boy, ready for a nap after all the excitement, didn't protest, but immediately stretched out on the quilt his great grandmother spread on the ground beside her chair. Prince lay down next to him.

Mandy made her way back to where Stephan waited with a length of nylon cord. She moved over close to him...close but not quite touching...and suddenly she found it hard to breathe. The laughter and shouts of the people around them grew muffled, and the only person she could see clearly was Stephan.

He took the extra step, moving next to her, placing his left leg against her right. Mandy heard a sharp intake of breath and wasn't sure if it came from her or him.

For a moment his gaze locked with hers and she couldn't remember why she'd ever thought of his eyes as glacial. Blue fire was more like it. The Texas sky in August when the heat beat down with no sign of a cloud and no hint of cooler weather.

"This may not be such a good idea," she said softly, giving him the chance to back out and knowing if he did, she'd die on the spot.

"Probably not," he replied and leaned over to wrap the cord around their legs.

His fingers brushed her skin lightly, only to the extent necessary to complete the task of binding them together. He was too much of a gentleman to use the opportunity as an excuse to touch her further, yet she almost groaned in her need for that touch.

When he finished and straightened, she noticed that his face was flushed and perspiration had beaded on his forehead and upper lip. The temperature had risen several degrees for her, too. She was aware of every nuance of his leg as it touched hers...the hard muscles, the dark wiry hairs. She even fancied she could feel the color of his tan.

He wrapped one arm about her for balance, and she did the same to him. His hand on her waist was firm and gentle and sent that temperature up even higher. His body was solid and real beneath her fingers, and she found herself wishing away his shirt, wanting to feel more of his skin.

"Ready?" he asked, looking down at her.

She nodded, even though she was pretty sure she wasn't even close to ready for this.

The starter's gun sounded.

"Step," he said as they moved out, then continued in cadence, "step, step, step, step." Amazingly they maneuvered without falling.

Laughter and shouts increased as other couples fell and tried to rise again.

"Hey, Steve, you should have come with me!" someone called, and Mandy looked up to see Carol and Bert Fenton pass them.

A fleeting thought...a wish?...darted through her mind. Had Carol really been heading toward Stephan a few minutes ago when he'd insisted she be his partner for the race? Or had Stephan just wanted her to do this with him, to have an excuse to touch and hold her?

Stephan increased his cadence and Mandy laughed. "You really like to win, don't you?"

He grinned at her. "Step, who, step, doesn't, step?"

In spite of their efforts, as they made the turn to go back, another couple ran into them, fell back and toppled to the ground. Mandy and Stephan teetered. He grabbed her, breaking her fall and pulling her on top of him as they hit the grass beside the path.

For a moment they lay tangled around each other, laughing.

The first couple struggled to their feet and continued on, but Stephan made no effort to rise.

"I'm sorry," she said.

"I'm not."

She lifted her head to look at him, and he was

smiling but no longer laughing. "We're going to lose the race," she told him.

"You said everyone's a winner as long as they have fun." He drew the tips of his fingers lightly down her arm, leaving a path of stimulated nerve endings that seemed to connect to every other nerve in her body and set them all to dancing in rhythm with the blood rushing past her ears and with Stephan's heart beating hard and fast against her breasts. "I'm having fun." His voice became noticeably hoarser. "Are you?"

"Yes," she whispered. "I am." The grass they lay on had been mowed the day before, and the bright green fragrance blended with Stephan's masculine essence and flowed around and through her, flooding her senses. Beneath her stomach, she could feel a stirring in the area of his groin, and that increased her own stirrings. "But we have to get up," she forced herself to say.

He wrapped both arms around her and slid them down her back to her waist. "Why do we have to get up? Why can't we just stay here for a day or two?"

Entwined with the blatant desire in his eyes was a sparkle that seemed to come from deep inside, and she realized with a start that he was teasing her. Stephan Reynard, the man who'd come to dinner in July in Willoughby, Texas, in a long-sleeved shirt, suit and tie was actually teasing her.

She giggled. She probably sounded like Stacy. She felt like Stacy…exhilarated, aware, young and totally entranced by these new feelings.

"If we don't get up soon, they'll think we're injured, and somebody will come and help us."

"Very well. We'll get up. For now."

The promise in his words and his eyes increased that exhilaration. Once again something stirred in a dark corner of her mind, something to do with a nebulous reason why she shouldn't be having so much fun. However, the thrill of being in Stephan's arms, of feeling his physical desire for her, of sailing on the wings of her own desire diverted her attention from that corner.

They scrambled around, encumbered by their legs bound together, and it occurred to Mandy that the process of rising would probably be a lot easier if they untied the cord...but she didn't suggest it and neither did he. Every movement created an excruciatingly tantalizing flash of flame that set off new fires in her body and increased the colorful whirlwind in her head.

When they finally stood, Stephan reached down to undo the cord that bound them. Again his fingers brushed her legs lightly, only a little beyond what was required to complete the action of untying their bonds. She rested a hand on his neck, against the vein that visibly throbbed there, and thought she would surely explode from the unfulfilled yearnings he stirred in her.

When the cord fell to the ground and Stephan straightened, neither of them moved away. Still they stood with flesh pressed against flesh, the connection unbroken.

He took her hand and squeezed, then released it. "I need to go for a short walk away from the crowd," he said, his smile slightly embarrassed. "Being so close to you has an effect on me that shouldn't be public."

For a moment she didn't understand why he wanted

to leave her, but then she remembered the stirring she'd felt against her pelvis.

"Oh! Yes, well, I'd better go check on Josh."

He laughed gently at her embarrassment. "I'll stroll about for a few minutes then get some more tea for us and your grandmother. After that race, I think I could use something cold."

"Cold. Right. Good." She cleared her throat. "They'll probably start serving the ice cream in a few minutes."

He touched her cheek briefly with the fingertips of one hand, then walked away.

In a daze Mandy wandered over to where she'd left Nana and Josh. Prince bounded up to meet her, barking excitedly, which woke Josh from his nap. Her son stretched sleepily and reached for her. Mandy picked him up and sat down on the quilt, cuddling him in one arm and stroking Prince with the other hand.

"Where's Stephan?" Nana asked.

"Oh, he's, uh, gone to get some more tea." She felt a flush rise to her face. Was Nana looking at her in a strange way? Her grandmother had always been unusually observant. Could she tell by Mandy's voice or the look on her face what had just happened? Could she read her mind? Mandy had often thought so when she was a child.

"Isn't that interesting?" Nana said, and Mandy froze. "The boy wouldn't drink his tea cold when he first came here, but I believe he's had a gallon today. People do change. And speaking of change, what do you think of your little sister's beau?"

"Her beau?" It took a moment for Mandy's mind to engage, to pull away from all the effects of the sensuous tumble in the grass with Stephan. "Oh,

Kyle! He seems nice. But young. They both seem awfully young.''

Nana chuckled. ''I was three years younger than Stacy when I met your grandfather. He moved to Willoughby during the summer, just before school started. I had a new pink dress with ruffles that my mother made me for the first day of school and I had my hair in curls. It was blond in those days.''

She smiled, and Mandy could almost see the young girl she'd once been.

The shadows around them had lengthened, and the people scattered through the park appeared subdued, moving more slowly, talking more quietly. A few feet away, a boy only a little younger than Kyle sat with his legs dangling over the edge of the highest part of the bank and tossed small stones into the water below, making soft plopping noises. The day had been glorious, but it was coming to an end, and Mandy's heart clenched painfully as she looked at her grandmother, at the wrinkles and white hair, the signs of age that masked the young girl inside who still remembered wearing a pink dress with ruffles.

''Eldon said I flounced into that schoolroom,'' she continued, telling a story Mandy had heard before but never tired of hearing. She knew that Nana enjoyed telling it, reliving her own glorious day that had lasted more than fifty years then ended abruptly two years ago. ''I don't believe I flounced, but that was always the story he told. Anyway, he said when I flounced in there in that pink dress with those blond curls, he knew he was going to marry me. And he did.''

Josh wiggled and Mandy realized she'd been holding on to him too tightly, as if she could hold on to this day, this moment when he still belonged to her and Nana sat beside her, when her family was almost intact.

She loosened her grip on her son, and he scrambled up. "Pins!" he called, and he and the dog charged off the quilt and into the grass, barking and shrieking happily in their usual chaos.

Mandy took her grandmother's hand in hers and noticed for the first time that her fingers were no longer completely straight, they were becoming knotted.

"It's a little arthritis," Nana said as if she could read Mandy's thoughts. "Nothing much."

"Enough to slow down your pie baking?"

"No, of course not! Just makes dealing at bridge a little slower."

Changes. So many, so fast, as if her world had been taken up in a Texas twister.

Prince barked from several feet away. A loud splash sounded, and she had only a second to think that Prince had likely jumped into the lake, chasing a stone thrown by one of the kids, before she heard Stephan scream, "Joshua! Stop!"

She looked up in horror to see her son leap from the bank into the deepest part of the lake.

Chapter Eight

Stephan dropped the three plastic glasses of iced tea and ran, sprinting as fast as he'd ever run in his life in spite of the fact that every movement seemed to be in slow motion as if in a horrible nightmare. Except this time the horror was in front of him, not dogging his heels. He'd seen Joshua's dog plunge into the lake, chasing something thrown by one of the boys. It hadn't occurred to him until too late that Joshua might follow.

As Stephan dove off the bank, he tried to somehow distinguish and remember the location of the ripples that marked the place where Joshua had gone under. But by the time he surfaced, his own ripples had obscured any left by the boy. Panic threatened to overtake him as he looked desperately in every direction, but he couldn't afford to panic. Josh's life depended on his ability to remain calm. Using every technique he'd learned through the years, he pushed aside that panic, forcing himself to be rational and unemotional.

He noticed peripherally that someone else hit the water right behind him, but he couldn't take the time to see who it was.

He plunged into the depths again, searching for any sign, but the murky water obscured his vision, and he was unsure exactly where Josh had disappeared.

He surfaced to take another gulp of air then saw Prince, his shaggy hair plastered to his body, rise from the depths, bark and dive under again.

Stephan followed him. The dog stayed close enough that he could see him even in the muddy water...and Prince took him straight to the small form flailing desperately and futilely as it sank toward the bottom of the lake. The dog deserved a steak a day for the rest of his life. Mandy was right. He was royalty.

As Stephan swam toward Joshua, he found he could no longer keep the tight rein on his emotions. His heart clenched painfully and hammered erratically, and it seemed an eternity of horror, watching the boy's movements becoming slower, of wondering if he would be too late.

He couldn't bear to think about losing this last link with Lawrence, this child who deserved all the happiness his father had missed, this boy who had somehow slipped past his guard and become entrenched in his heart.

He couldn't think about that possibility, but he couldn't think about anything else.

After what felt like hours, but could only have been seconds, he reached Joshua.

He grabbed the slight, motionless form, pulling Josh against him with one arm, then stretched the other toward the surface of the lake and pushed upward with all his might.

They burst into the light. Stephan took a deep gulp of the air, then tucked the boy into his side and with his free arm swam as hard as he could for the bank. Prince swam alongside, and the dog seemed somehow as anxious as he was.

As he reached the bank, a sea of outstretched hands waited to take Joshua. Stephan had an irrational urge to hold on to the boy, as if by letting go of him he would somehow lose him.

"I'm a doctor!" someone shouted. "Get out of the way!"

Stephan let them take Joshua from him, then boosted himself and Prince up onto the bank just as the doctor, an older man, pushed through the crowd.

"Joshua!"

Stephan turned to see Mandy emerging from the lake. She must have been the person who'd jumped in behind him.

He helped her onto the bank, then wrapped his arms about her, holding her close, and the two of them stood looking on helplessly while the doctor pushed on Stephan's small, motionless chest. Mandy cried openly, and Stephan was grateful for the water dripping from his hair that hid the moisture in his own eyes. Even Prince, who sat beside them, was subdued, looking from the boy to Mandy and back again, whimpering.

As the doctor pushed, lake water gushed from Joshua's mouth. Once. Twice.

Prince whimpered again, or maybe it was Mandy or himself or all three of them. No one in the crowd made a sound.

Joshua coughed.

The doctor pushed again.

Joshua coughed again, sucked in a deep breath and began to wail.

Mandy sank to the ground beside him. "Thank God, thank God!"

"Give him some air, Mandy," the doctor protested, pushing her back and lifting Joshua in his arms. "It's okay, little guy. I'm gonna take you over to one of these picnic tables and get a closer look, if these fools will get out of my way."

As the doctor examined a screaming Joshua on the red-and-white-checked tablecloth spotted with barbecue sauce, Mandy comforted her son and Stephan stood watching. He'd never felt so completely helpless and frightened as he had in the last few minutes.

If the purpose behind Mandy and her family asking him to move in with them had been to give him the opportunity to form emotional attachments, they had succeeded admirably. He hadn't realized how much he cared for Joshua until he'd almost lost him. He would have been devastated if anything had happened to that child. Worse than devastated. It would have been like losing Lawrence all over again.

He would have given his own life to save Joshua.

And Joshua wasn't the only person he'd become attached to. Somehow Mandy had slipped under his defenses, too. He'd been intrigued by her passion the first time they'd met and now he understood why. He was capable of that same passion. He'd discovered that today. He wasn't sure if he could ever get all those emotions back under control. He wasn't even sure if he wanted to.

He wrapped an arm about Mandy and held her

against his side as she trembled. If he could, he'd take on her fear and pain. If he could, he'd bring only happiness to both her and Joshua.

He couldn't, of course. By his presence, he'd complicated their lives and could only make them both unhappy.

He had an obligation to his country to return their prince to them, but Mandy was right. He couldn't force Joshua to grow up the way he and Lawrence had. Even with him there to intercede, it would not be the life Joshua enjoyed now.

Heaven help him, he cared for both of these people, for the entire family. The best thing he could do for all of them would be to leave.

A part of him screamed that he had to do his duty, that Lawrence's son should know of his birthright.

But another part reminded him of the birthright Joshua had now, of all the things the boy had that he and Lawrence had never had in spite of their wealth and royal ancestry: love and passion and Fourth of July picnics and a dog named Prince, just for starters.

He felt a foolish, selfish ache at the thought of leaving the big old house that didn't have a single gold fixture or imported rug or painting by a master yet housed more treasures than he'd ever known.

However, the fact that leaving was going to cause him pain was inconsequential. He'd known from the beginning that was what happened when one formed attachments, when one let one's emotions have free rein. If he couldn't have avoided becoming attached to Joshua, he should at least have had more restraint where Mandy was concerned.

He shouldn't have made it worse by giving in to his desires and kissing her, by insisting she run that three-legged race with him just so he could touch her, by deliberately stumbling so he could hold her. He shouldn't even be standing here right now with his arm around her, trying to absorb her fears.

If he genuinely cared about these people…and he did…the kindest thing he could do was get out of their lives as fast as he could.

The doctor stepped back from the table. "You folks take this young man home and put him to bed, and he'll be right as rain tomorrow. Probably won't want to go swimming for a while. You may even have trouble getting him into a bath tub. He could be one smelly kid after a few weeks." He chuckled at his own humor.

Mandy reached down to pick up Joshua, who continued to cry loudly as if to prove he now had his breath back. Her arms were still trembling as she wrapped them around him and Stephan wasn't sure she could carry him.

Or maybe he just wanted an excuse to carry the child one last time.

"Let me take him," he offered. "Hey, big fellow, want to sit on my shoulders and go for another race?"

Joshua's tears abated a couple of degrees. Stephan lifted him onto his shoulders, and he calmed to intermittent snuffles.

A warm glow washed over Stephan. He had the ability to calm the boy.

Mandy reached up and patted Josh's soggy bottom, then hugged Stephan. "Thank you," she said. "Thank you for saving our Joshua's life."

A peculiar sensation rather like fireworks exploded in Stephan's chest. Not only had Mandy credited him with saving Joshua's life, but she'd said *our Joshua*.

Her spontaneous expression told him she thought of him as having a claim on the boy, that she was willing to share her son with him, that she accepted him as a part of Joshua's life even if it was only for a day. Stephan was amazed at the happiness such a small remark could cause. He was amazed at how important all of it was to him.

"Prince deserves some of the credit," he said, a little uncomfortable with so many rampant emotions. "He took me right to Joshua."

Mandy leaned down to pet the wet dog. "You're a good dog, Prince. However, I'm not forgetting that you got him into this mess in the first place. You can't chase everything anybody throws!" But her words lacked anger.

She took Stephan's arm. "Let's go home. I'm awfully tired."

Home. Her home, but not his. He didn't want to go to his home, but he needed to, as quickly as travel could be arranged. This entire situation had gone completely out of control. He needed to get away, get some perspective.

Josh was asleep from exhaustion by the time they pulled into the driveway, but midnight found Mandy still wide awake. Too much had happened that day for her to be able to relax and sleep.

She gave up trying, slipped on a robe and went downstairs. Maybe if she sat outside for a while and absorbed some of the serenity of the summer night she could relax enough to sleep.

She stepped out onto the porch into the cool, night-scented darkness and knew immediately that Stephan was there even before she saw him sitting in the glider. She could sense his presence as surely as if he'd touched her.

"Couldn't you sleep, either?" he asked.

She shook her head. He scooted over to make room for her beside him. She hesitated. She ought to unfold one of the lawn chairs. She shouldn't sit next to him. But she wanted to, needed to.

As she sank down beside him he wrapped an arm around her shoulders. It felt so good and so right, even though she knew it was so insane.

"I'm exhausted. I should be able to sleep," she said.

"So should I, but I can't."

They sat in silence for several minutes. A chorus of katydids blended with a tree frog's song and an occasional raspy burst from a cricket. An owl hooted its eerie call. A breeze rustled the cottonwood leaves with their distinctive clicking sound. The peace of the Texas night stole over Mandy, but Stephan's body beside her kept her from relaxing completely, kept her heart pounding in double time and her blood rushing. It was a delicious tension, but still a tension.

"I was very worried about Joshua today," Stephan finally said, his voice low and resonant, a part of the night that surrounded them.

She laughed softly and said, "You're so good with understatements."

He chuckled. "Yes," he agreed, "that was most assuredly an understatement. I couldn't have borne it if anything had happened to him."

"You care about him."

He was silent for a long time. "I do. He's a very special little boy."

Stephan had been unusually quiet since the incident

at the lake. She sensed that something was going on with him, that he was close to making a decision about Josh's future, but she hadn't pressed him. She wasn't sure she wanted to know what it would be.

She couldn't believe, after everything that had happened, that he would insist that Josh go with him to Castile. On the one hand, even if he'd decided to go away and pretend Josh didn't exist, it was too late. Things had changed that could never be put back the way they were.

One of those things was the way she felt about Stephan. At the picnic they'd acted like lovers, like they were just any man and woman having a good time, enjoying each other in all the ways a man and a woman could enjoy each other—laughing, talking and touching.

She understood only too well how Alena had become involved with Lawrence even though she'd known the hopelessness of such involvement. Right now, in spite of knowing that Stephan held nothing but problems and pain for her, she wanted to be with him for as long as possible.

Another thing that had changed was Stephan. After today he couldn't deny that he had feelings…for his brother, for Josh, for her. However, she suspected from his actions that those feelings frightened him, that he wasn't quite sure what to do about them, how to stuff them back into a box.

As though he could read her thoughts, Stephan shifted in the glider so that he faced her, lifted one hand to her cheek and gently turned her toward him. For a moment his eyes searched hers as if looking for reluctance, giving her time to pull away from what they both knew would only make the inevitable harder to accept.

She gathered her courage to do just that, but her body betrayed her. Instead of rejecting him, her lips parted in invitation.

His mouth descended to hers, the kiss immediately passionate and hungry...greedy for all that could be savored in this midnight where neither belonged to any world except that which existed between their lips. For this moment Stephan was not the prince of a faraway kingdom, a wealthy, powerful man who could only bring pain. He was simply the man who held her against his broad chest, the man who had the strength to pull her son from death's door, yet caressed her back and neck with hands as gentle as the velvety night that wrapped around them.

His lips on hers were warm and smooth, and he tasted of the mint of his mouthwash and barbecue sauce from the picnic and a desire so strong it could override all common sense. His kiss set off explosions in far-reaching parts of her body, setting her on fire and making her yearn for more of him.

His heart pounded wildly against her breast in perfect rhythm with her own, and she wanted to lose herself in that primitive rhythm, forget all the reasons why she shouldn't.

Just the way Alena had forgotten.

With every ounce of willpower she could muster, she pushed away from him and leaned back in the glider, looking across the yard, anywhere but at him.

"You're leaving, aren't you?" she asked as soon as she could catch her breath.

"Yes," he said, his voice so soft the single word

seemed to ride in and be a part of the breeze that filtered through the trees.

"Without Josh."

"Without Joshua," he confirmed. "You're right. I can't subject him to any degree of what Lawrence and I went through. He's happy with you. In a few years, when he's older and able to understand, we will urge him to spend some time with us in order to learn our ways...and his duties, should he decide to assume the throne."

She nodded. It was more than she'd dared to hope for. So why did it make her feel as if she had a huge, aching hole in her heart?

Because it meant she'd never see Stephan again, never feel his lips on hers again or see his eyes light up like the summer sky when he laughed.

"When are you leaving?"

"If Joshua is all right, I'll make arrangements tomorrow."

She rose abruptly. "Well, I'd better go on up to bed now. Get some sleep so I don't nod off in church tomorrow."

"Good night, Mandy."

"Good night, Stephan."

Mandy walked back into the house that had always been her refuge before, a place where she felt warm and loved and totally safe. But at this moment she didn't feel any of those things. She felt lonely and sad, the way she had when Gramps died.

Stephan had admitted that she'd been right about Josh. Well, she'd also been right about him. He'd changed their lives and brought nothing but unhappiness.

* * *

Stephan remained in the glider on the Crawfords' front porch. There was no point in going up to bed. He wouldn't sleep.

He was doing the right thing, the smart thing, the noble thing, and all he felt was miserable.

He clenched his fists in his lap—the same hands that had only minutes before held and caressed Mandy's soft body. Damn it, he'd known better than to get involved! He had no one to blame for his pain but himself.

For the first time he understood Lawrence's actions.

At least he knew he wouldn't be leaving Mandy with his child.

But if he stayed around her much longer, he wasn't so sure that wouldn't happen.

He was leaving here just in time.

An errant breeze brought him the scent of some local flower, the same one he'd smelled in his room the first evening he'd come here, and the scent was Mandy…wild and sweet and an integral part of this land.

This time the person he cared about wasn't leaving him; he was leaving her…because he cared about her.

Because he loved her.

He wasn't sure when or how it had happened, but suddenly he was sure he did.

He wasn't leaving just in time at all. Looking back, he realized that from the moment Mandy had walked into that kitchen it had been too late to leave "just in time."

In the predawn hours of Sunday morning, Stephan moved about the Crawfords' guest room, packing.

Though it was still dark out, he could feel and smell dawn approaching, and with it came the bittersweet memory of the mornings he'd shared on the front porch with Mandy.

He couldn't go down today. He was fairly certain Mandy hadn't gone out for the dawn ceremony, either. Every morning he would hear her quiet steps going down the stairs, and he'd follow behind her.

He'd tried not to listen this morning, but he hadn't been able to stop himself, and he hadn't heard that familiar tread.

He'd decided last night as he lay in bed tossing and turning, his body and his heart achingly aware of Mandy in her bed just one floor beneath him, that, even if he wasn't able to make the necessary travel arrangements today, he'd leave Willoughby and go back to the hotel in Dallas.

He closed his suitcase and looked around the room that had somehow, in one week, become more familiar than the one he occupied at home. This room—this entire house—had a welcoming aspect to it, a soul.

It had plenty of defects. It creaked at night, the water pipes groaned when he showered, and it became as hot as Hades during the afternoon. His home, on the other hand, was a beautiful palace with a staff on call to fix the slightest creak or groan, and even in the summer, the sun never blazed down the way it did in Willoughby, Texas.

He was going to miss Willoughby. He was going to miss the entire Crawford family with their casual lifestyle, their easy acceptance of a stranger into their midst, their peculiar foods, some so hot they brought the Texas sun into his mouth, and so much love they were able to take it for granted.

Most particularly, he was going to miss Mandy Crawford with her hair that captured that Texas sun, her smile as wide as the summer sky, eyes that mirrored the trees in her front yard and skin as soft as the evening breeze. She was like this country…hot and fierce and tough and gentle, taking his breath away and scorching him one minute then soothing his soul the next.

He set his suitcase by the door, then returned to wait in the wingback chair for daylight before he went down. The room, with all his things packed away, was the same as when he'd come—the antique furniture, its finish warmed by the people who'd made it a part of their lives, the lacy doilies that Nana had crocheted, the open windows already lightening with the new day.

It was as if he'd never been there. When he left, Mandy and her family, like this room, would go on with their lives the same way, as if he'd never been there.

But he wasn't at all sure he was ever going to be the same.

From the stairs below he heard Mandy's footsteps. Dawn had passed. His last day here had begun.

Mandy pinched off a piece of biscuit dough, rolled it between her palms and plopped it into the pan, did the same with the remainder and slid them into the oven. Bacon sizzled and popped in the big iron skillet when her mother turned it. Silverware clinked as Stacy set the table. Josh sat in his high chair, beating a spoon on the tray and babbling in his part-English, part-Josh language while Nana tied on his bib.

The morning was clear and bright. A mockingbird perched in the elm tree outside the kitchen window and serenaded them with its changing melodies.

Life was good. It would soon be back to normal, almost the way it had been before Stephan came.

This morning she had forced herself to lie in bed until daylight, avoiding the dawn ritual that Stephan had shared with her. After he left she would feel different about it. In a week or so. Maybe a month. Or two.

"Good morning, youngest daughter." Her father came in and tossed the large Dallas Sunday newspaper onto the table. "Good morning, oldest grandson, oldest daughter and only mother." He went to where Rita stood at the stove and kissed her on the back of the neck. "And a special good morning to you, wife."

"Aren't you chipper?" Rita lifted a piece of bacon onto the paper-towel-covered plate and smiled at her husband as he poured himself a cup of coffee.

The look that passed between her mother and father was private and special, speaking of a shared life, a shared bed, possibly shared lovemaking. It was a look Mandy had seen many times over the years, a look that always gave her a sense of warmth and security, reminding her she was the daughter of parents who loved each other and had created her in love.

Today it made her feel lonely.

Today it wasn't enough to be that daughter. Suddenly she wanted to be a part of that kind of relationship. Her heart ached with the knowledge that she would never share that look with Stephan.

"Good morning." As if he'd appeared from her thoughts, Stephan walked into the room. Instead of his shorts and knit shirts, he was dressed in his slacks and white shirt. The tie and coat were missing, but they'd be close by. For all intents and purposes, he was already gone.

The mockingbird had stopped singing and the sun seemed dimmer.

"Stee!"

Stephan leaned across the table and rumpled Josh's hair. "Glad to see you've recovered from your first swimming lesson."

"Good morning, Stephan," Dan said. "Going to church with us?"

"No. I appreciate the invitation, but I can't. I've decided to return home today."

The room became completely still. Even Josh, as if sensing the adults' tension, was quiet.

Mandy had thought she couldn't feel any more depressed about Stephan's leaving, but hearing the formal announcement pounded home the reality.

"What about Josh?" Dan asked.

"Right now I believe his interests are best served by remaining here. In the future, when he's older, I'd like to work out some schedule of visitation."

Dan looked to Mandy. She gave him a single, brief nod to let him know she had accepted Stephan's decision.

"That seems fair," Dan said. "But you don't need to be in such a hurry to leave. You're welcome to stay as long as you like."

"We've enjoyed having you here," Nana added. "I was counting on you to stick around at least long enough to get Dan going on installing that air-conditioning.''

Dan chuckled. ''Mama, you're the one who said for years we didn't need it.''

''I can change my mind. You make good pies, too, Stephan.'' She winked at him. ''We're going to miss you. Like Dan said, no need in hurrying off.''

''I need to get back to Castile and advise them of my decision. I think it best I leave today. I have my bag already packed.''

Everything he said brought Mandy's mood lower and lower.

He looked at her and she saw the agony in his eyes.

Alena had told her how much Lawrence hated to leave her. At the time, she'd thought Lawrence had lied, that he wouldn't have left her if he'd cared so much, if it had hurt so much. Now she knew he'd told Alena the truth. Because he cared for her, he'd left her. He could neither ask her to share a life so lonely as his nor could he abandon his duty and stay with her. So he'd left Alena. Just as Stephan was leaving her.

The teakettle gave a shrill whistle. ''Your water's hot,'' Rita said. ''And breakfast is almost ready.''

''Excellent. Thank you.'' Stephan took down a cup and made his tea.

Dan settled in a chair and opened the paper. ''That photographer who came down from Dallas took a picture of some of us over by Sam Walker's big old smoker yesterday morning. Let's see if they printed it.''

''A photographer?'' Stephan's voice was stiff. ''I had no idea there were reporters at the picnic.''

''Oh, just one real nice lady and a photographer.

Said they wanted some human-interest filler stuff. They do that every year and never use any of it. They probably left before you got there." He rustled through the pages then folded some back. "Here it is. Uh-oh. I hope this doesn't cause some problems."

A chill gripped Mandy at her father's words. She smashed the last egg onto the side of the bowl too hard, and it oozed onto the counter top.

"What is it?" Stephan asked.

Dan lifted the page for everybody to see. The story had a collage of photos of the barbecue pits, people eating, kids playing...and a picture of Stephan with Josh on his shoulders and Mandy looking up at both of them adoringly.

Stephan moved closer and took the paper. "The caption says Visiting Father Saves Son from Drowning."

"What!" Mandy exclaimed.

"It's just a misprint," her father soothed. "We left out of there so fast, whoever took the picture didn't have time to question us, so he asked somebody else, and whoever it was gave him the wrong information."

"One of those gossips just had to start it up again! Oh, Lord, I hope nobody sees this!"

"Don't swear, sweetheart," Dan said. "It's going to be all right. Nobody pays any attention to these stories."

Someone knocked on the front door.

Chapter Nine

For a moment everyone in the room remained frozen in place, even Joshua.

It couldn't have lasted more than a few seconds, but Stephan seemed to have eternity to look at these people and to know that he'd changed their lives irrevocably. He could tell, by the peremptory sound of the knock, by the hairs standing on end on the back of his neck, by whatever sixth sense he'd gained from dealing with the press over the years that a reporter…or reporters…stood on the Crawfords' front porch.

Dan rose. "I'll get it."

Stephan handed him the newspaper. "Let me," he said grimly. "I imagine it's me they're looking for. Someone in the press has likely seen my picture and recognized me."

"I'll go with you." Mandy wiped her hands on a tea towel.

"No, you stay here."

She plopped the towel onto the counter and faced him squarely. "No. I live here. Whatever's going on, I'll have to deal with it sooner or later."

She was right about that. He'd be gone in a few hours, leaving her to deal with the events he'd set in motion...including the way they felt about each other.

Together they walked to the front door, his hand at the small of her back, a token of his need to support her as well as to touch her again, one more time before he left. Not that one more or a hundred more would ever be enough.

Through the screen door Stephan could see a boy— a young man—with a notebook and pen in one hand and a small tape recorder peeking from his shirt pocket.

"Hi," the young man said. "I'm Garrison Randolph with the *Willoughby Weekly News,* and I wondered if I could ask you a few questions about the rescue yesterday."

"Not now," Mandy replied. "We're getting ready for church."

"There's nothing to tell except what was already in the paper," Stephan said. "Joshua Crawford fell into the lake while chasing his dog who was chasing a stone tossed in by another child. I saw the incident, dove in and pulled the boy out. He's fine today, getting ready to have breakfast. So, if you'll excuse us—"

"Is it true this guy's the father of your child?"

"No!" Mandy exclaimed indignantly. "Joshua's adopted!"

"I am not the child's father," Stephan said, adding his calm denial to her outburst. He'd had a lot more experience dealing with the press than she had and knew it served no purpose to become upset. "I have never been to your country before last week, and that can be verified. There's no story here. Now, if you don't mind, we were preparing to have breakfast."

The boy wavered, and Stephan almost breathed a sigh of relief that it had been so easy.

Almost.

A van pulled up to the curb in front of the house and stopped—a van bearing the logo of a Dallas television station. A female reporter and camera crew emerged.

Stephan slammed the wooden door, shutting out Garrison Randolph and the new arrivals.

Mandy bit her lip. "We went through this when I came back to Willoughby with a baby and no husband. Not the reporters, of course, but the other part, about Josh's father. Some of the people here—" She wrapped her arms about herself and shook her head slowly "—some of them like to gossip, and they kept asking me and my family snide questions. I went to the doctor whose nurse is the worst gossip of the bunch and I told the doctor I needed a complete physical. His nurse saw the records. She saw I'd never had a baby. Then I went to the library, made a photocopy of the adoption decree and left the original in the copier for someone to find. It took a while, but the talk died down. After you leave, it will again. Everything will go back to the way it used to be." The desperation in her voice told him she was trying to convince herself.

Another knock sounded on the door.

"Please leave," Stephan said loudly. "We're having breakfast."

"Prince Stephan, is it true you're in this country to

claim your love child?'' It was a woman's voice, apparently the television reporter.

Stephan closed his eyes and drew a hand across his forehead. ''I'm sorry, Mandy. No matter what I do or say, no matter how soon I leave here, I'm afraid things are never going to be the way they used to be for your family.''

Garrison Randolph's face appeared at the open window beside the door. ''Prince? We have a prince right here in Willoughby? What country are you the prince of? Does that make this Joshua a prince?''

The phone rang.

Stephan closed the window while Mandy answered the phone.

He turned toward her and saw a look of horror spread over her face as she held the receiver to her ear. He extended his hand, and she gave it to him without protest.

As soon as he pressed the instrument to his ear, he recognized the strident voice of Jean Taggart. ''...that picture! How dare you try to claim our grandson for your own? He's a prince and you're nothing but trash, living down there in that old house that's about to fall down around you and your worthless family.'' Stephan could feel the hot blood rising to his face. His hand clutched the phone so hard it hurt. He hadn't liked the crude, smarmy Taggarts when he'd met them. Even so, he was amazed and furious at how vicious the woman was being while she believed Mandy was still on the phone. ''We're going to file a lawsuit and take that boy away from you! When we get through with you and your family—''

''That's enough,'' Stephan interrupted, and was pleased to hear a surprised gasp on the other end of the line. Obviously she'd recognized his accent. "If you even think about filing a lawsuit against the Crawfords or doing anything else to hurt them, my family will ruin you. I'll personally see to it that you lose everything you own and your name is so blackened, you'll never again be able to walk through the door of that country club you're so proud of. If I hear from the Crawfords that you've so much as phoned them or had your lawyer phone them, even if it's not an abusive phone call, even if it's to wish them a Merry Christmas, you can forget about ever being invited to a function at the palace."

He slammed down the receiver, heart pounding, adrenaline pumping.

Passion. He had certainly learned about it, found it within himself, and he wasn't at all certain how long it would take to unlearn it, to bury it deep inside again. He wasn't even certain that was possible.

Mandy laughed shakily. "That ought to take care of the Taggarts."

He grinned ruefully. "Only for the moment. If they talk to anybody who knows anything, they'll learn that the only threat I can actually follow through on is the one not to invite them to the palace, which I wouldn't do anyway. Even if I could do any of the others, it would provoke a national incident. We can only hope that when the real story comes out in the newspapers and they see you weren't to blame for the mistaken identity of Joshua's father, they'll settle down a bit. Though when they find out Joshua is still with you rather than in Castile, they may try to cause trouble."

"Prince Stephan, does your brother's death have anything to do with your visit over here? Now that you're the heir to the throne, are you reclaiming your son?''

Stephan moved back to the door. ''Please give us a few minutes, and I'll be out to talk to you,'' he called.

He took Mandy's hand and led her to the other side of the room where the intruders on the porch couldn't hear. ''Go on back with your family and I'll deal with these people. They won't leave until they get a story.''

''What are you going to tell them?'' Her eyes searched his, begging him to make this problem go away, to rescue her family the way he'd rescued Josh yesterday, and with all his heart he wished he could.

He sighed and shook his head. ''I'll tell them the truth. It's the only way to get rid of them and have any chance of mollifying the Taggarts. I'm sorry. I never meant to upset your life.''

''You must have known something like this could happen when you came here.''

''No. I thought it would be a simple matter.'' He didn't know what vicious things Jean Taggart had said to her a few minutes ago before he took the phone, but he refused to add to the woman's insults by telling Mandy what the Taggarts had said about her family…and what he'd believed before he met her. ''I thought we'd be able to work out something with Joshua and I'd leave immediately. I don't suppose I gave much thought to the consequences to you and your family. That was before I met you, before you became real people to me…before I learned to care about all of you.''

The knocking came again. ''Are you going to take the boy's mother back to Castile with you?''

The words hit him with the force of a fist in the solar plexus. He gazed down at Mandy. "Am I?" he asked quietly, and suddenly the thought of getting on that plane without her, of entering that cold palace without her, of spending the rest of his life without her, came crashing down on him. He knew he'd face all sorts of problems if she went with him, but right now he couldn't think of a single one. Whatever they were, they wouldn't be as bad as the ones he would face without her—the loneliness, the pain of loss, the empty days stretching ahead for the rest of his life. Nothing could be worse than that.

But he knew how devoted she was to her family. Maybe, if he asked her to come for a short visit, she could manage that, and then...

He couldn't think about *then* right now. Too much was going on. He could only deal with the moment. "Come with me to Castile. You and Joshua. For a visit. Give this some time to die down."

She looked up at him, and in the clear light of Sunday morning that streamed through the windows and left her vulnerable to the world, he could see in her eyes the battle raging in her heart. She wanted to go with him. Nevertheless, he wasn't surprised when she shook her head.

"I can't," she whispered. "I know everything's changing and it'll never be back the way it was, and it's not just because of you. Stacy's growing up. She'll graduate from high school and go on to college and then get married and leave home. Nana's getting older. Dad's talking about retiring, and he's turning over more and more of the hardware business to Darryl. And now we're going to be hounded by reporters and everybody will know Josh is a prince. But none of that changes the fact that this is my home. It's the only place I've ever felt safe and loved. I left once, and it almost wasn't here to come back to. I wasn't even here for my grandfather's final days. What if I left now and Nana died? Or Mom or Dad? I can't. I love them so much.''

''And I love you that much.''

She looked as surprised as he felt. He hadn't known he was going to say the words until they actually spilled out, hadn't known he would have the courage to tell her.

He lifted a hand to stroke the smooth skin of her cheek. That elusive scent of Texas flowers washed over his senses. The sounds of the reporters on the doorstep became muffled and faraway. Only he and Mandy existed in the entire world. Only she could destroy that world.

''I didn't know I could love anyone the way I love you,'' he said. ''You've opened a Pandora's box of emotions inside me. I love you and Joshua and your entire family. Now that it's all out, I don't know how to handle it. I need you to show me how to deal with all this love.''

She caught his hand with hers and pressed her lips to the palm. ''I love you, too, Stephan.'' Her words and her touch thrilled him, set off a volcano in his chest. However, the sadness in her eyes brought him crashing back to reality. ''But that doesn't change anything. I can't go to Castile with you,'' she said.

He nodded, squaring his jaw resolutely. ''I understand.''

Suddenly he was five years old again and another nanny was leaving, while his mother admonished him to remember he was a prince and princes didn't cry.

Of course, he wasn't being left behind this time, but that was a technicality. The various nannies had chosen another, less-stressful job, a husband, an ailing relative. Mandy had chosen her family and Willoughby, Texas.

Her fingers on his trembled and her eyes were deep wells of pain and regret. "You're a good man. You'll make a good king."

"Mama!"

He looked up to see Stacy with Joshua in her arms, coming through the dining room toward them. "All the noise is upsetting him," she said. "He wants you."

Stephan leaned down and kissed Mandy's cheek. Her hair brushed his face, and he felt the warmth of Texas and Mandy, smelled the flowers that belonged to Mandy and to this land that she loved.

"Go to your family," he said, pulling away from her. "I'll do what I can to get rid of the reporters. When you return from church, I'll be gone. If you need me, I'll be at the hotel until I can make arrangements to return to Castile. You can send the media over there. I'll deal with them."

She looked at him for a long moment, and he knew that he would never again see a tree or a blade of grass without thinking of Mandy Crawford's eyes. She was a part of this state and a part of her family, and she wouldn't be the same without either of them.

Joshua called to her again, and she turned away and went to her son.

Stephan left the house and went out to face the reporters.

As soon as their van turned the corner onto their street coming home from church, Mandy saw that another television vehicle sat where Stephan's rental car had been for the past week. His car was gone. He was gone.

She'd known he would be, but the sight of the empty space sent shock waves of despair through her body. Somehow it felt all wrong, made everything feel all wrong, even though her family was with her and they were going home.

Dan guided their van into the driveway, and the crew ran over with cameras and microphones.

"You stay here," he directed. "I'll handle them."

But Mandy shook her head. "Stephan said they wouldn't go away until they got their story. I'll give it to them. I'll tell them whatever they want to know. We'll get this whole thing out in the open and pretty soon people will get bored with it and go on to the next celebrity divorce or political scandal for their entertainment."

She climbed down from the van, then turned back to get Josh. The rest of her family came to stand beside her, as they had always done. She told Josh's story in stark, factual details, all the facts that were necessary to placate the media and as little as possible of the emotional struggles behind those facts. Stephan would, she thought, have been proud of the way she handled it.

When they left, she went inside her home with her family to the Sunday roast cooking in the crock pot. They'd have to deal with the media for a while. They might even have to deal with the Taggarts.

But eventually things would return to a semblance of normality. Eventually she'd have her life back.

As she looked at the extra plate Stacy had, from

habit, set on the table, she wasn't so sure. A large part of her life would soon be halfway around the world in a cold, lonely palace. She had a warm, wonderful home and family, but her heart felt like that cold, lonely palace.

Chapter Ten

Fall was in the air. Mandy sat on the top step of the porch, having her first cup of coffee Saturday morning and savoring the crisp feel and the scent that always reminded her of the clear amber of a glass of tea. Afternoon temperatures were still in the eighties and only a few trees sported an occasional yellow leaf, but already changes were underway.

The sun rose a minute or two later every day, and Mandy determinedly remained inside until it had crested the horizon. By next spring she would surely be ready to resume her dawn ritual, but not yet. Right now she couldn't bear the thought of watching the sky gradually lighten and catching that elusive scent of faraway lands when Stephan was in one of those faraway lands.

Since he'd left three months ago they'd spoken on the phone every weekend, always brief check-in calls. He talked to the whole family, including Joshua, who'd begun to utter coherent sentences upon occasion.

His father, Stephan said, was having health problems and was relegating more and more of the authority to him. He, in turn, sought his sister's assistance. Schahara, he said, had a much better aptitude for running the country than he did. But he would do his duty.

Always unspoken, but hanging in the air, was the assumption...the hope...that one day Josh would assume those duties.

He inquired as to everyone's health and well-being and asked about the weather. He maintained contact with the heir to the throne. That was all.

The front door opened behind her, and for one brief instant Mandy's heart fluttered, forgetting for a moment and expecting Stephan to come out to join her.

"Good morning, sweetheart."

"Good morning, Nana."

The older woman eased down onto the step beside Mandy and for a few minutes they sat in comfortable silence.

A car turned onto their street, and Mandy, immediately on full alert, anger and adrenaline pumping, half rose to dart inside at the sound of the motor. When the circumstances of Joshua's birth hit the news, her family had been besieged by reporters from every branch of the media. After the first month, the flood had dwindled to a trickle, mostly from the tabloids. It had been almost three weeks since they'd been bothered, but Mandy's conditioned responses were still with her.

The car drove past without stopping, and Mandy

sank back down, shaking her head. "Guess I'm still a little jumpy."

Nana laughed softly. "I can understand why you would be, after the past few months."

"It was awful, wasn't it? No privacy at all. Living in the spotlight. But things are pretty much back to normal now, except the way some people still act so silly around Josh."

"You mean as if he's royalty or something?"

Mandy laughed at her grandmother's facetious comment. "Something like that. I just want him to have a normal, happy life, the way I did. But things are not as bad as I was afraid they'd be. Most of the people around here are starting to take it in stride. I still worry that the Taggarts will do something crazy, though."

"They might. They were both mean little kids, and they haven't changed much over the years. Raymond was a year older than your dad, and he used to steal Dan's lunch money and his pencils and anything else he could get his hands on until the first day of the second grade when he tried to take Dan's new notebook that had a picture of Mickey Mouse on it. Dan fought back, and Raymond didn't know how to take that. He's a bully. Dan called his bluff and now Stephan's done the same. Jean and Raymond may try something, but I'd say there's a pretty good chance they won't. Try not to worry too much. Worry doesn't help anything, you know."

Mandy leaned forward, head in her hands, elbows on her knees. "I know. I don't. Not much, anyway. I'm just so grateful that, for the moment at least, everything's back almost the way it used to be."

Except for that big, empty hole in her heart.

"Nothing's ever the way it used to be. You still miss Stephan, don't you?"

Mandy straightened. "Why do you say that?"

Nana patted her leg. "Because you're my grand-daughter, and I know you almost as well as I know myself. Don't you worry about that, either. Anyday now the right man will come along and sweep you off your feet."

"I know." But she didn't know any such thing. Mandy couldn't imagine ever loving anyone but Stephan. The thought of another man touching her, holding her, kissing her was revolting.

"Stephan cared about you. I could see it in his eyes, in the way he looked at you."

Mandy shrugged. "He cared as much as he could. It's just that he's not an ordinary man, someone who gets up every morning and goes to an office. He's a prince, and he has duties and responsibilities."

"He was in as much pain as you were that last morning. I halfway expected him to ask you to go to his country with him, to be his Cinderella."

"Oh, Nana, you're such a romantic! He asked me to go with him until all this mess with the media died down, but of course I couldn't."

"Why not?" Nana didn't seem very surprised, and Mandy wondered how much she'd already guessed.

"I can't leave here. This house, all of you, even this town where some of the people are pretty weird, this is my life. You know how unhappy I was when I went to Dallas, and that was close enough I could come home on the weekends."

"With all of Stephan's financial resources, I'm sure you could come home any weekend you wanted to from Castile."

Mandy shook her head. "If he didn't have so much of what you delicately call 'financial resources' and if he wasn't a prince and didn't have so many duties, things might be different. Are you forgetting how unhappy Alena was? And her family had plenty of those 'financial resources.' So did Lawrence, and look how disastrously that relationship turned out. All that money only made her unhappy."

"Sweetheart, having money didn't make Alena unhappy. Jean and Raymond Taggart are mean, vicious little people. They were the same way when they were dead broke. They're the ones who made Alena unhappy. Money gave them more power to be meaner to more people, but it didn't change the basics. As for Lawrence, I never met him, but if he was anything like his brother, I think he would have married Alena and claimed their child if he'd had a chance."

Mandy tossed her cold coffee into the yard and stood. She knew what Nana was saying was logical, but she also knew it wasn't entirely practical. Money did cause problems and divisions, no matter what her grandmother, always the romantic, wanted to believe, and talking about Stephan and the impossibility of any kind of relationship with him because of those problems only increased the pain.

"I'm going in for another cup of coffee. Want me to get you one?" Mandy asked.

"Thank you." Nana gave Mandy her cup. "And there's a small carton of real cream behind the orange juice."

"Nana! What about your cholesterol?"

"The carton's almost empty. There's no point in stopping now."

With a sign of resignation at her grandmother's

stubborn streak, Mandy went inside and refilled the cups, then returned to the porch. The sun was bright on the horizon now but with the subdued brightness of fall rather than the brashness of summer.

"Stephan doesn't have a front porch," she said, taking her seat again. "When he told me that, I had a surge of sympathy for him. Isn't that silly, feeling sorry for a man who has a fifty-room palace, just because it doesn't have a front porch? But it kind of puts things in perspective. Our house may not be a palace, but I've got a front porch and a grandmother to share it with."

Suddenly a horrible thought struck her. "Are you sick?" Was that why she wasn't worried about her cholesterol? Because it no longer mattered?

Nana smiled. "No, I'm not sick. I plan to be around for a while yet." Her eyes narrowed shrewdly. "Is that part of the reason you wouldn't go to Castile? Because your grandfather died while you were in Dallas? Do you think I'll die if you leave home again?"

"Of course not! But it is true that a lot of bad things happened when I was away from here. Gramps died. Alena died."

"And just as many good things happened. Darryl married Lynda. Joshua was born. Gramps would have died whether you'd been here or not. He had an aneurysm. You couldn't have prevented that."

"I know."

"I'm not sure you do, at least not in your heart." Nana set her cup on the porch and took Mandy's hand between both of hers. "Our lives keep changing, just as surely as summer changes to fall and then to winter and spring again. You couldn't have held on to your grandfather and kept him here one second longer anymore than you could make the summer last one second longer.''

"I could have been here with him for his last days."

"Would that have really mattered? You were with Alena for her last days. Did that make it any easier?''

"Nana, if I didn't know better, I'd think you were trying to talk me into leaving home.''

"I am. If I'd known before he left here that Stephan asked you to go with him, I'd have tried to talk you into it then!''

"This is my home. You're my family. I can never leave. I don't want to leave.''

Nana released Mandy's hand, picked up her cup and leaned against the porch post. "I wish you could have known my grandmother.'' Mandy relaxed. Nana was going to tell another story and get off the subject of Stephan and of her leaving home.

"She's the wonderful lady that granddad built this house for,'' Nana continued. "Grandmother Langston was from a big family in Atlanta. She knew all the right people and went to the right parties. Granddad came to Atlanta on a business trip and met my grandmother at a dance. It was two more trips before he convinced her to marry him and move to Texas. She loved her family, she loved the big-city life of Atlanta, and in those days Dallas was pretty small and uncivilized by comparison. Willoughby was the middle of nowhere. But she loved Granddad with all her heart. Back then, a trip from Atlanta to Willoughby took a lot longer than a trip from the United States to Castile does now. Cars were a new invention and neither reliable nor speedy. Roads were nonexistent, so she didn't get to visit home but once a year. Grandmother said she never stopped missing her family and Atlanta, but she never once regretted marrying Granddad and coming here to live.''

Mandy shifted uncomfortably. For once, Nana's story didn't make her feel all warm and fuzzy inside. It made her feel jumbled and confused.

"It doesn't matter, anyway," she said quietly. "Stephan only asked me to go to Castile until the media storm blew over. It wasn't anything permanent, and he hasn't mentioned it again.''

"When he does—"

"He won't.''

"When he does, I want you to think about something. It's not this house and the ground it sits on that you love. It's the people who live in it with you. This is only a building, and it could be as cold and lonely as Stephan's palace if we didn't have each other. We could sell this place and move into a brand-new home and still be happy. You could even turn Stephan's palace into a home filled with love.''

Her grandmother's words echoed through Mandy's head the rest of the day. She knew Nana was right, but she couldn't bear to think about leaving her home for any reason.

The palace was colder than Stephan remembered, the nights longer and the starch in his shirts stiffer.

Or maybe it was just the contrast to Texas.

It was only October. Castile would get much colder as winter came on.

Stephan hung up the phone after his weekly call to the Crawfords. He lived for Sunday afternoons, for the moment when the phone would be lifted in a big old house across the ocean and he'd hear Mandy's voice. For those few moments of contact he was warm and content again. But when it was over, the chill once more pervaded his soul.

"Talking to your Texas lady again?"

Stephan looked up to see that Schahara had entered the room. She flopped inelegantly onto the antique red velvet sofa and lifted one leg, draped in khaki trousers. Schahara refused to give in to the royal-dress-code demands, except on formal occasions.

"Yes," he said. "I was talking to Mandy as well as Joshua, Dan, Rita, Vera and Stacy. Anyday I expect Prince to get on the line."

"Speaking of that dog, do you realize you've been moping around like a depressed bassett hound ever since you came home?"

Stephan picked up an imported vase from the table next to his chair. The deep blue glaze made the material seem almost translucent, and the gold tracings added shine. He had no idea of its worth, but it was probably more than the Crawfords' entire house. Money-wise, at least. He could smash the vase against the marble floor, and no one's life would be altered for better or worse. But the Crawfords' house brought them happiness, provided a gathering place for all that love.

He set the vase down and had no yearning to pick it up again.

He had a strong yearning to return to the Crawfords' old house.

"Yes, my dear sister, I do realize I haven't been quite on top of things lately. I simply don't know what to do about it."

"Go see her. Talk to her. I've never known you to be a quitter before."

Stephan rose from the uncomfortable wooden chair and scowled down at his sister. "Schahara, sometimes you're an incredibly pushy woman."

"All the time, brother dear. All the time. It's why I do such a good job helping to run this country." She grinned up at him.

Stephan stalked out of the big, empty room—empty despite the elegant furnishings that crowded every square foot—and went into the wide, empty hallway. His sister meant well, but he knew Mandy would never come to Castile with him. She was as firmly rooted in Texas as one of those live oak trees in her front yard.

He'd thought a thousand times of going to see her one more time, asking her one more time. But that would only make the loneliness worse. Surely the longer he was apart from her, the more it would ease. Although, that easing process had not yet begun.

He paused at the door of his father's library as all the rational logic he'd been trying to drum into his head evaporated into the mist of those emotions Mandy had roused from their dormant state. Maybe he should talk to the king about the possibility of making one more visit to Texas.

Why? his good sense asked. So he could see Mandy again, perhaps even hold her in his arms again, then have her yanked away again? Reopen the wound?

Though it wasn't as if that wound had even started to heal.

Before he could think about it anymore, he knocked twice and pushed open the door, not waiting for an answer.

The king looked up from the big, overstuffed chair

where he sat, then looked away immediately, but not before Stephan saw that his face was swollen and tear stained.

Had the king developed allergies? The ancient, leather-bound books that reached from floor to ceiling on all sides of the room did have a musty odor.

"Father, I need to talk to you about something."

"Not now." The king's voice cracked.

Stephan crossed the room and stood next to the king, peering down at the big man who'd always seemed omnipotent. For the first time he noticed that the king's hair was thinning on top and that the hands that clutched the arms of the chair were becoming wrinkled. "Are you all right, sir?"

"Certainly."

Stephan moved around the chair to stand in front of his father. "You've lost weight and you have dark circles under your eyes. So does the queen, on the rare occasions when she comes out of her room." A thought struck him, a thought too outrageous to even consider.

"Please leave the room. I did not invite you to enter."

Stephan wavered, so accustomed to obeying the orders of the king that such obedience was almost automatic.

Almost. He'd been away long enough for other habits to make inroads. He thought of the easy way the Crawfords had gone from room to room in their open house. Other than the bedrooms, no place was considered private or off-limits. Orders were tempered with love.

"I didn't mean to interrupt you," he said. "Of

course I'll leave. I just wanted to tell you that I'm planning another trip to Texas.''

The king's head jerked upward, and Stephan was stunned to see the ravages of grief so clearly written on the man's face. Perhaps his outrageous thought wasn't so outrageous, after all.

"You've been crying," he said, unable to keep the shock from his voice.

The king glared at him for a moment, then looked away. "My eldest son is dead." His words were bald and uninflected. "That's a difficult situation to endure, even when you're a king."

His legs suddenly rubbery, Stephan squatted on the floor in front of his father. "You mean it bothers you that Lawrence died?"

"Do you think I have no feelings?"

"Yes," Stephan answered quietly. "Yes, that's exactly what I think. That's what you taught Lawrence, Schahara and me—to have no feelings."

"A monarch cannot afford to have feelings. Ruling a country should be done with the brain, not the heart." He sighed. "That's not always easy to do. Would you please leave now? We'll discuss this trip you'd like to take at a later time."

Stephan stood, his whole world reeling crazily around him. "Very well. But I have one question. Did you and the queen ever...did you love Lawrence, Schahara and me?"

"Love you?" For a moment the king's voice softened. "Of course we did. We do." He reached for a bottle of brandy and poured himself a healthy drink. The conversation was ended.

Stephan left the room and stood leaning against the

door for a long time, trying to catch his breath, both literally and metaphorically.

His parents had wasted all the years of his life. He, Lawrence and Schahara could have had their love, and his parents could have had that of their children all this time, but they threw that away because it wasn't acceptable for royalty. He didn't want to do what they had done, didn't want to be like them. He didn't want to lose one more minute of Joshua's love or of Mandy's.

No matter what the king said, Stephan was going back to Texas.

Chapter Eleven

"Would you hand me that wrench?" Dan asked, and Darryl selected the requested item from the pile of tools on the bathroom floor.

From the hallway Mandy watched the struggle between man and plumbing, between her family and their home that seemed to be in constant need of repair. This latest leak was no worse than the hole in the roof last month or the driveway that still hadn't been redone, it was just one more in a never-ending procession of problems. Over the past few days it seemed her family was constantly doing something to the house...cleaning, repairing, rearranging, their efforts unusually frantic, as if they faced some kind of deadline.

"All these pipes need to be replaced," Darryl said.

"I know. As soon as I retire, I'll have more time to fix up this old place."

Since her talk with her grandmother a week ago, Mandy had been thinking about a lot of things. Her family's recent flurry of efforts and now her father's comment had coalesced those thoughts. "Dad, you don't want to spend your retirement working on this old house."

He and Darryl looked up from their work under the sink. "What is it, sweetheart? We'll be through here in a minute." He checked his watch. "Damn! Sorry, Mandy. We're going to be late opening the store. It's already nine o'clock."

"Can I help, and you can let Darryl go?"

"That'll be great."

Mandy switched places with her brother and squatted in the floor next to her father. "Dad, I've been thinking."

Her father grunted as he tightened a fitting.

"Like I said, you don't want to spend your retirement keeping this place from falling down."

"It's not that bad. A couple of years of full-time work and I'll have it good as new."

"Do you want to sell this house and get something newer, something with a dishwasher and central air and no stairs and a small yard?" she hurried on, pushing the words out while she still had the courage to say them, to offer to give up the home that had always been her sanctuary, her anchor, the center of her life. "If you do, it's okay with me. Wherever we live will be great as long as we have each other." As she spoke the words, she knew they were true, and something inside her relaxed with the knowledge that she could stop holding on so tightly to the pieces of her life that weren't crucially important after all.

Dan tested the fitting, then sat back on his heels and laid his wrench carefully on the tile floor. "What is this, baby doll? What's going on?"

"It's just that things are changing and maybe it's time we changed with them."

"What things?"

"Nana has trouble with the stairs, and Stacy's leaving for college next fall, and we have all these empty rooms that still have to be cleaned, and you and Mom should be able to retire and relax, not spend your time on this place. We could get one of those all-brick ranch-style houses in the new addition south of town. Wall-to-wall carpeting, central heat and air, built-in microwaves, dishwashers and garbage disposals, two-car garage. Make everybody's life easier." And it would be a house where Stephan had never been, where she had no memories of sitting on the front porch with him, of eating dinner with him across the table, of his lips touching hers so gently yet with such a blazing passion. That would surely make it easier to forget, if she wasn't reminded of him at every turn.

"I see you've given this some thought."

"I guess I have. I didn't realize how much until now, but I guess I have."

"It wouldn't be the same as living here."

"Yes, it would. As long as we have each other, yes, it would."

Mandy's father studied her quietly for a long moment. "I'll tell you what, we'll have a family meeting and discuss this after lunch. Right now I need to get to the store."

Another layer of tension dissolved. She'd have a few hours to really think about all the ramifications of her rash proposal. In her heart she knew she'd done the right thing, but the thought of leaving her family home still required some getting used to.

"I think I'll take Josh to the park this morning. It's a perfect day for it."

"No, that's not a good idea. I need you to stay here. I'm, uh, expecting a delivery."

Mandy looked at her father quizzically. He sounded unduly concerned that she should stay home. "Nana can accept it."

"No, she's going to get her hair done."

Mandy shrugged. "All right. We'll stay here."

Just as well. If she was going to leave this place, she wanted to memorize every board, every blade of grass, every cracked windowpane and groaning water pipe.

No delivery had arrived by eleven. Nana was still at the beauty shop, Stacy had left to "hang out" with Kyle, and Rita had insisted on taking Josh along when she took Prince to the vet. Mandy sat on the front porch in the glider, preparing her lessons for the following week.

She looked up at the sound of a car stopping in front of the house. Her immediate reflex was to run into the house and close the door, avoid the media, but she reminded herself this was probably the delivery her father had expected.

A tall male figure climbed out of the driver's side, and her heart did a somersault but then vaulted back down to the floor. Good grief. When was she going to stop seeing Stephan in every tall man? This was a cowboy in a wide-brimmed hat, blue jeans, denim shirt, big belt buckle and boots.

She went to the front of the porch as he came down the walk, his face shadowed by the hat brim. As he approached, he suddenly swept off the hat and bowed. "Howdy, madam."

Mandy blinked once in confusion, then burst into delighted, soaring laughter. "Stephan?"

"Yes, madam."

For a few moments she could only laugh in amusement, delight, relief and a thousand other tumbling emotions. When she could catch her breath, she said, "Somehow it's not quite the same when spoken with your accent. And it's ma'am, not madam! Take my word for it, you don't want to call a woman in Texas a madam."

Stephan sighed. "I'm not sure I'll ever be able to master this Texas language."

For a moment she gazed at the face that had filled her dreams for the past three months, the face that exactly filled that empty hole in her heart. "We didn't expect you! Come on in. Would you like some iced tea? Everybody's gone right now, but they'll be back." She was babbling, something she did a lot of around him.

"I wanted to surprise you, I don't want any iced tea, and I know everybody's gone. We arranged it that way."

"You arranged it that way? Dad knew you were coming?" That's why he'd been so anxious that she not leave home this morning.

"Yes, your father, your mother, Nana, Stacy, Joshua and probably Prince. I wanted some time to talk to you alone."

"All right." The two words came out barely above a whisper. Was he going to ask her again to visit Castile? Was she going to go? "The, uh, media. You were right about them. They've stopped coming." If he did ask, she wanted it to be for reasons other than the protection of Josh and her.

"Can we sit down?"

"Oh, yes, of course." She stepped back and motioned to the glider.

He sat on one end and looked at her expectantly.

"Josh has really grown," she said, fumbling for something to say as she sat beside him in the glider. His thigh pressed against hers, and his scent was that of a different soap than when he'd been here, but the underlying masculine essence was the same. Memories of the last time they'd sat there together flooded her mind, and she could almost feel his lips on hers. "Stacy and Kyle are quite an item. But you already know all that from talking to us on the phone, don't you?" She was babbling again in an effort to hide her nervousness and only making it more obvious.

"I've missed you," he said quietly.

"Me, too."

"But I understand why you don't want to leave here."

She started to tell him that was no longer true, that only a couple of hours ago she'd offered to sell this house and leave. Still that wasn't the same as leaving her family, leaving Texas.

And he hadn't asked her to, anyway.

"I'm not good at conveying my emotions," he continued. "I've had very little practice, but there are some things I need you to know." His eyes were as deep and brilliant as the Texas sky, and the thought flashed through her mind that, no matter where he was, he'd always have that bit of Texas with him.

"I believe I've already told you my father has been relegating more and more duties to me," he went on.

"I thought his health was failing, and I suppose in a way it is. One evening I walked in on him in the library drinking brandy and crying. He's upset because of Lawrence's death." He paused and shook his head slowly as if in amazement. "I couldn't believe it. I was astonished to discover that my parents have feelings, too, that they actually did love us, even though they were always careful to hide it."

"What a horrible, stupid thing to do!"

"Yes, it was. They wasted their lives and part of ours. Since that happened, I've watched them both, going through the proper motions, pretending they're fine, and I feel incredibly sorry for them."

"You're a kinder person than I am, Stephan Reynard. I think that's an outrage!"

"It is. But it's over and done, and I can learn from their mistakes." He took her hand between both of his. "I've talked to my parents and to my sister. I've told them I don't want to be king, not even if it's just until Joshua grows up, not if it means I'll lose the person I love. The people I love. Though my father disapproves, Schahara will be pleased to take over the duties of running the government. It's time our country acknowledged the equality of women. We need her to bring us into the twenty-first century. Mandy, I love you with all my heart. I've been decidedly unhappy without you. I want to move to Texas and marry you, if you'll have me."

For a stunned moment Mandy wasn't sure she'd heard right. "You want to move here? You want—"

"I'm aware that being a prince isn't exactly a marketable job skill. I've always dreamed of being an architect. I wanted to build affordable, comfortable housing in our country. I can do that here just as well, starting with your house. I have all sorts of ideas for renovating, without compromising the integrity of the original structure and…''

The whole world was spinning crazily around Mandy. Bright, vibrant colors of the future swirled and blended so fast she couldn't quite comprehend any of them. She held up a shaky hand. ''Wait a minute. Slow down. You want to move here, live in this house?''

''Yes. Isn't that what you want?''

''It is. Of course it is. But I just talked to my father about selling the place and getting a new one.''

''We could do that, if that's what you want, or we could make this one like new.''

Was it possible she could have her house, her family and Stephan? Mandy wanted to laugh, sing, dance. ''Have you talked to my dad about this? You said he knew you were coming today.''

''I had to ask your father for his permission to marry you before I could ask you.''

Mandy gazed at him in shock, unsure if she should be insulted, flattered, angry or amused. She chose the last. ''And what did my father say?''

''He said he'd welcome me as a son-in-law, but that I was on my own in getting you to agree to leave here.''

''You didn't tell him you were planning to come to Texas to live?''

''No, I didn't feel it was appropriate to mention that part, until I knew what your answer would be.''

She swallowed hard. ''My answer?''

''Your answer.'' Stephen slid from the glider onto one knee on the weathered wooden boards of the porch and took her hand. "I love you, Mandy Crawford. Will you consent to becoming my wife?"

The rainbow of swirling colors and confusion shifted and settled into place. Her world came into focus, full and complete. Stephan loved her and wanted to spend the rest of his life with her. She'd never have that empty hole in her heart again.

She smiled. Then burst into tears. Then laughed.

Stephan looked puzzled and distressed.

"These emotions," she explained. "Once they're out, you never know what they're going to do." With the fingertips of her free hand, she traced the familiar contours of his face, savoring the knowledge that those contours would become even more familiar through the years. "Yes," she said. "I consent to becoming your wife."

A huge smile spread over his face like the sun cresting the horizon at dawn. He pulled her to her feet and into his arms. His lips descended to hers, and she gave herself completely, with no need for reservations. There would never again be a need to hold back from loving Stephan.

Over the sound of her heart beating wildly, she could hear a mockingbird's song. How peculiar that the bird had stopped singing when Stephan left, and only now started again.

Or maybe she just hadn't been able to hear its song while Stephan was away. In order to survive his absence, she'd had to close up a portion of her soul. Now it was again open to the world and all its beauty.

With a final kiss Stephan drew away from her but only a few inches. His eyes were heavy-lidded with passion, his breathing rapid and his voice husky when he spoke. "Before we get married, before we spend a single night together in this house, we must have air-conditioning installed.''

"Before? It's October! Even Texas cools down in the fall and winter.''

"I have a feeling it's going to be summer all year in our bedroom.''

She felt herself blush even as she shivered in anticipation. "You have a point. But—'' She bit her lip, bit back the words she knew she had to say.

"But?'' he repeated. "Is there a *but?* You don't like the idea of air-conditioning?''

"I love the idea of air-conditioning. I <u>love the idea of living here with you and my family</u>.'' She looked into his eyes so full of love and trust. She didn't have to make the concession. He'd agreed to stay with her.

Yes, she did have to make it, because she loved him.

"We don't have to live here. I'll go to Castile with you. As much as I love this house and Texas and my family, without you I've been miserable. Wherever we are, as long as we're together, will be home for me.''

Stephan studied her in silence for a long moment. When he finally spoke, his voice was full of wonder. "When you agreed to be my wife, I was filled with so much love and happiness I didn't think it was possible to know more of either of those emotions, but you've just expanded both exponentially. Thank you.''

"Hey, cowboy,'' Mandy teased, "you may have the emotions right, but you've got a ways to go learning the language. *Exponentially* is not exactly a romantic word.''

"All right, let me rephrase that. You have filled

my heart with a bounty of joy I would have never believed possible.''

''That's an improvement.''

''I would like to continue to be a part of my country's future.''

Mandy felt a twinge of disappointment and fear, but only a twinge. What she'd said had been true. Wherever she was, as long as she had Stephan's love, she would be happy.

''However,'' he continued firmly, ''I want to live here. I love this house and Texas. There's something about this land that's so untamed and free and—'' he looked about him, then grinned ''—hot. I want Joshua and our other children to know both their heritages. I want them to go to barbecues and play balloon toss and get the insides of their mouths burned off then soothed with your marvelous iced tea. Then I want them to see the palace and the crown jewels and meet my parents, who, perhaps, will do better with their grandchildren than they did with their children. Perhaps we could divide our time between the two countries.''

''Yes,'' she agreed, and her happiness had just multiplied exponentially, too. ''We could do that. I know you have duties to fulfill.''

''Duties which Schahara will gladly share.''

She stretched upward and kissed his cheek. ''Have I told you lately how much I love you?''

''No, I don't believe you have.''

''I love you, Stephan Reynard, Prince of Castile.'' She looked him over from head to toe...the slight indentation in his hair from wearing the hat he now held in one hand, the fit of the Western-cut shirt across his broad chest, the belt buckle that he'd put on upside down so the panhandle was at the bottom and Houston at the top, the stretch of taut denim over his flat abdomen, the boots with pointed toes. "But I confess, I think I love you best as the Texas prince."

He kissed her forehead. "No matter where we are, you'll always be my Texas lady."

Arms wrapped about each other, they entered the big old house that would see another generation of children descended from that great-great-grandmother Mandy had never known who'd left her home in Atlanta to come to Texas.

The addition of air-conditioning would be nice, though.

Especially at night, when she and Stephan would be sharing the bedroom upstairs, Nana and Gramps's old room.

* * * * *

Silhouette ROMANCE™

VIRGIN BRIDES

Your favorite authors tell more heartwarming stories of lovely brides who discover love... for the first time....

July 1999 GLASS SLIPPER BRIDE
Arlene James (SR #1379)
Bodyguard Jack Keller had to protect innocent
Jillian Waltham—day and night. But when his assignment
became a matter of temporary marriage, would Jack's hardened
heart need protection...from Jillian, his glass slipper bride?

September 1999 MARRIED TO THE SHEIK
Carol Grace (SR #1391)
Assistant Emily Claybourne secretly loved her boss, and now Sheik
Ben Ali had finally asked her to marry him! But Ben was only
interested in a temporary union...until Emily started showing him
the joys of marriage—and love....

November 1999 THE PRINCESS AND THE COWBOY
Martha Shields (SR #1403)
When runaway Princess Josephene Francoeur needed a
short-term husband, cowboy Buck Buchanan was the perfect
choice. But to wed him, Josephene had to tell a *few* white lies,
which worked...until "Josie Freeheart" realized she wanted
to love her rugged cowboy groom forever!

Available at your favorite retail outlet.

THE FORTUNES OF TEXAS

*Membership in this family has
its privileges...and its price.
But what a fortune can't buy,
a true-bred Texas love is sure to bring!*

Coming in November 1999...

Expecting... In Texas

by

MARIE FERRARELLA

Wrangler Cruz Perez's night of passion with Savannah Clark
had left the beauty pregnant with his child. Cruz's cowboy
code of honor demanded he do right by the expectant
mother, but could he convince Savannah—and himself—
that his offer of marriage was inspired by true love?

THE FORTUNES OF TEXAS continues with
A Willing Wife by Jackie Merritt,
available in December 1999 from
Silhouette Books.

Available at your favorite retail outlet.